The Three Investigators

The Mystery of the Fiery Eye

7

by Robert Arthur

Random House ⌂ New York

A RANDOM HOUSE BOOK
Originally published by Random House in 1967.
Revised edition, 1984.

www.randomhouse.com/kids

Library of Congress Cataloging in Publication Data
Arthur, Robert.
The Three Investigators in The mystery of the fiery eye.
(The Three Investigators mystery series ; 7)
Previously published as: Alfred Hitchcock and The Three Investigators
in The mystery of the fiery eye.
Summary: Three junior detectives solve a mystery involving a collection
of antique busts, a legacy, a strange letter, and a red ruby.
[1. Mystery and detective stories.] I. Title. II. Title: The mystery of the fiery eye.
III. Series.
PZ7.A744Th 1984 [Fic] 83-22991
ISBN: 0-394-86407-7 (pbk.)

Printed in the United States of America
6 7 8 9 0

Contents

Introduction

Welcome, mystery lovers. Join me and The Three Investigators in another suspenseful and mystifying case. This time they tangle with a mysterious message, a strange inheritance, a sinister man from India, and other surprises that you'll soon discover. All I can say at this point is that if you love mystery and danger, you've come to the right place.

If you're already familiar with my friends, turn right away to Chapter 1 and start reading. If you've never been introduced before, let me do the honors. Jupiter Jones, Pete Crenshaw, and Bob Andrews call themselves The Three Investigators. Their motto is "We Investigate Anything." And they really do. So far they've investigated a green ghost, a haunted castle, a whispering mummy, and other slightly bizarre situations, to say the least.

Jupiter Jones is known for his remarkable powers of observation and deduction. Pete Crenshaw is the athletic member of the firm. Bob Andrews is studious and skilled at research. Together they make a great team.

Their home is in Rocky Beach, California, a few miles from Hollywood. Their headquarters is in The Jones Salvage Yard, which is owned by Jupiter's aunt and uncle, Mathilda and Titus Jones.

Which is enough introduction. On with the story!

—Hector Sebastian

The Mystery of the
Fiery Eye

A CALL FOR THE THREE INVESTIGATORS ————— 1

IT WAS a busy day at The Jones Salvage Yard. Mrs. Mathilda Jones was keeping her nephew Jupiter and his friends Bob and Pete on the jump. Seated in a wrought-iron garden chair outside the neat little cabin that served as her office, she watched the three boys working with an eagle eye. They were unloading the big salvage yard truck of the assorted objects Titus Jones had brought back from his most recent buying trip.

"Jupiter!" she called now. "All those statues on the truck! You boys bring them over here and stand them in a row on this table. We'll make a nice display of them."

She was referring to a number of plaster heads of famous people which lay carefully bedded down on some canvas in the back of the truck. Technically they were not really statues, but busts. About half life-size, they showed only the head and shoulders. They were the kind of sculptures sometimes seen on pedestals in museums and libraries.

Jupiter, Pete and Bob scrambled up into the truck and stared at the busts. To the boys they didn't look like anything anyone would want very much. Altogether there were thirteen of them, and they all looked a bit grey from many years of gathering dust. The name of the person each represented was chiseled on its square base.

"Julius Caesar, Octavian, Dante, Homer, Francis Bacon, Shakespeare," Jupiter read off some of the names. "These seem to be all famous men."

"Augustus of Poland," Bob read. "I never heard of him."

"Or Luther or Bismarck," Pete added, pointing to two very stern-looking busts.

"But you've heard of Queen Victoria," Jupiter said. "And Washington, Franklin and Lincoln."

"Sure," Pete agreed. "Well, let's start with Washington." He bent down to pick up the bust of George Washington. "Oof!" he gasped. "It's heavy!"

"Be careful there, Pete!" called Mrs. Jones. "That's a very valuable and artistic statue. I'm planning to charge five dollars for it!"

"I'll get down, then you hand it to me," Jupiter said.

Pete got down on his knees in the back of the truck, and carefully lowered George Washington into Jupiter's arms. Jupe hugged him tight and staggered backwards. Gingerly he lowered the bust of America's first President to the table. Then he mopped his forehead.

"Aunt Mathilda," he said, "I think we should wait for Hans or Konrad to move these busts. Pete and I might drop one."

"Yes, indeed, you might," agreed Mrs. Jones, who had been watching every move. "And there would go five dollars! All right, Jupiter, you boys are excused for now. You can go have a club meeting, or whatever it is you do."

Some time back, Bob, Pete and Jupiter had formed a puzzle-solvers club, which they had later turned into the junior detective firm of The Three Investigators. However, Mrs. Jones had never quite grasped the fact that, though they still solved puzzles and entered contests for fun, their real interest these days was in solving genuine mysteries that came their way.

Mrs. Jones knew that Jupiter had a workshop section, fitted up with various tools and a printing press, back in a section of the yard which was hidden from sight by piles of building materials. What she didn't know was that they also had fixed up a headquarters for their firm of The Three Investigators, close to the workshop.

Headquarters was an old mobile home trailer that Mr. Jones had been unable to sell because it had been damaged in an accident. He had given it to Jupiter to use for a meeting place with his friends. Over the last year the boys, with the help of Hans and Konrad, the sturdy blond Bavarian yard helpers, had piled all kinds of junk around the trailer. Now it was completely hidden from sight and could only be entered through certain secret entrances.

Inside Headquarters was a tiny office equipped with a desk, telephone, tape recorder, filing cabinet and other necessities, and next to it was an equally small laboratory and a darkroom for developing pictures. Almost all the equipment had come in to the salvage yard as junk, but had been rebuilt by Jupiter and the other boys.

The three were about to head for Headquarters now when the other salvage yard truck, the small one, turned in through the gate. Konrad was driving and Titus Jones, a small man whose enormous moustache seemed the largest thing about him, sat beside him. Hans, the other Bavarian brother, was riding in the back of the truck with the load.

The truck stopped and Mr. Jones hopped out. The boys could see that the truck was loaded with a number of curious black objects known as dressmakers' dummies. These were made of black cloth over a metal frame, shaped to be about the size of a woman, but with a metal stand for feet and no head. Once almost every household had had one, and the lady of the house fitted her handmade clothing to it. Nowadays, however, you seldom saw one in use.

Mrs. Jones leaped to her feet, clutching her hair.

"Titus Jones!" she cried. "Have you gone out of your mind? In the name of goodness and mercy and sweetness and light, how do you expect to sell a truckload of old dressmakers' dummies?"

"We'll find some use for them," Titus Jones said, his composure unruffled. Mr. Jones was a very unusual junkman—he bought anything that interested him, not just things he knew would sell. And one way or another, he usually sold them again at a tidy profit.

"Jupiter, put your mind to what possible use an old dressmaker's dummy could be," his uncle instructed.

"Well," Jupiter said promptly, "it would make a great target for an archery club to shoot arrows at."

"Mmm." Titus Jones considered this. "Not bad, not bad. Keep trying. Ah! I see you started to unload my fine collection of plaster busts. An artistic and unusual purchase, if I do say so."

"At first I couldn't imagine what you bought them for," Mathilda Jones said. "But now I think I know how to get rid of them. As garden ornaments! They'll look very nice in people's gardens, perched on a column among the flowers and shrubs."

"I knew I could count on you, Mathilda," Titus said. "The very thing! Hans—Konrad—finish unloading. Be careful you don't chip them."

He sat down in the shade, got out his pipe

and started to light it as Hans and Konrad began lifting down the plaster busts.

"Those heads," he said. "Found them at an old place in a canyon in the hills. Grand old house. The owner died. All the furniture and rugs were sold before I got there, unfortunately. Nothing left but some odds and ends nobody else wanted—these busts, some books, a sun dial, some garden furniture. So I bought them."

He fell silent, puffing on his pipe. Jupiter, Pete and Bob took the occasion to slip away. In a moment they were back in their workshop section.

"Whew!" Pete sighed. "I thought your aunt was going to keep us working all day, Jupe."

"She would have if she hadn't been afraid we might drop one of those plaster heads," Jupiter replied. "Aunt Mathilda can't bear to lose money on a deal."

"What shall we do now?" Pete asked. "We haven't any mystery to investigate. Let's get out those maps of old ghost towns in the desert we're going to explore some day."

"Or we could work on that contest that offers a trip for two to Hawaii as first prize," Bob suggested.

"Well—" Jupiter began. At that moment a red light, mounted on a board over their printing press, began to blink.

"Look!" Bob yelled. "A phone call!"

"It might be someone wanting a mystery solved," Jupiter said hopefully.

Pete had already slid back the piece of iron grillwork that leaned against the opening of a large pipe behind the printing press. He crawled inside the large corrugated iron pipe which led, partly underground, through a tangle of junk to the hidden mobile trailer. The boys called this secret entrance Tunnel Two. Bob and Jupiter followed him. Pete pushed open a trap door at the other end and they all climbed up into the tiny office of Headquarters.

The telephone was indeed ringing. Jupiter snatched it up.

"Hello!" he said. "Jupiter Jones speaking."

"Hi, Jupe," said a hearty male voice, which they all could hear through the loudspeaker attachment that Jupiter had rigged up. It was Hector Sebastian, a detective turned mystery writer. He had become the boys' adviser and friend. When Mr. Sebastian called, it usually meant he had a case for them.

"What a pleasant surprise," said Jupiter. "What can we do for you?"

"I hope you aren't too busy right now. The son of a friend of mine is in town and he needs help. I think you and your friends are just the ones to help him."

"We'll be glad to try, Mr. Sebastian," Jupiter said. "What is your friend's problem?"

"Someone has left him something valuable," Mr. Sebastian said. "Unfortunately he has no idea what it is or where to find it. He's staying at the Hotel Imperial in Hollywood. Why don't you meet both of us there tomorrow morning at ten? Then he can tell you all about it himself."

TROUBLE WITH
MR. GELBERT_____ 2

"TERRIFIC!" Pete exclaimed. "Mr. Sebastian has a new case for us."

"A boy who has been left something valuable and doesn't know what it is or where to find it," Bob added, frowning. "It sounds pretty mixed up to me."

"The more baffling it is, the better," Jupiter said.

"We'll need a car to drive us over to Hollywood," Pete put in. "I'd hate to drive up to the Hotel Imperial in the old truck."

"I am phoning the Rent-'n-Ride Auto Agency now," Jupiter told them, starting to dial, "to tell them we will need the Rolls-Royce and Worthington tomorrow morning."

Some time ago, Jupiter had won the use of a genuine, gold-plated, antique Rolls-Royce, complete with chauffeur, in a contest. The car had been invaluable to them in their career as investigators, for distances in southern California are great, and it is almost impossible to cover them except by car. Of course, sometimes the three borrowed the salvage yard's small truck, with Hans or Konrad driving. But for a visit to the Hotel Imperial in Hollywood, a truck was hardly dignified enough.

"Hello," Jupiter spoke into the telephone. "May I speak to the manager, please? . . . Hello, Mr. Gelbert, this is Jupiter Jones speaking. I wanted to tell you I will need the Rolls-Royce, with Worthington, tomorrow morning at nine-thirty."

They were surprised to hear the man at the other end say, "I am sorry, but that will be impossible. Your thirty days' use of the car has expired."

"Golly!" Pete groaned in dismay. "We haven't been keeping track. The thirty days ran out while we were back East tangling with the mystery of Skeleton Island."

But Jupiter was speaking into the telephone again.

"According to my figures, Mr. Gelbert," he said, "the thirty days still have some time to run."

"But they don't!" Pete whispered loudly. "The thirty days ran out. He's right."

The First Investigator waved his free hand at them. The manager of the rental firm was speaking again.

"I'm afraid you're wrong," he said firmly.

"Mr. Gelbert," Jupiter said in a dignified voice, "I believe we have a difference of viewpoint here that needs to be straightened out. I'll be at your office in twenty minutes to discuss the matter."

"There's nothing to discuss!" The man sounded annoyed now. "The time is up. Come down, but it won't do you any good."

"Thank you," Jupiter said. He hung up and turned to the others. "We have to get our bikes and ride downtown."

"But he's right!" Pete protested as they crawled out through Tunnel Two. "Thirty days is thirty days."

"Not always," Jupiter said mysteriously. "Leave the talking to me."

"We'll leave it to you, all right," Bob agreed. "We haven't anything to say. I think we're wasting our time."

Jupiter would say nothing more. They rode out through the main gate, then half a mile down the shore road into the heart of Rocky Beach. Off to their left the Pacific Ocean gleamed blue in the sunshine, its surface dotted with boats. To their right rose the Santa Monica mountains, brown and jagged.

The Rent-'n-Ride Auto Rental Agency occupied a corner on the main street. The Three Investigators parked their bikes outside and walked in, Pete and Bob rather reluctantly following Jupiter.

They were shown into the manager's office. Mr. Gelbert, a stout, red-faced man, scowled as he saw them.

"Well?" he asked Jupiter. "You won our contest and you had the use of the car for thirty days. Now what makes you think you can keep on using it? Can't you count?"

"Yes, sir," Jupiter said politely. "I've tried to be very accurate in my counting, Mr. Gelbert."

From his pocket he took a small notebook and an envelope. He took a folded piece of paper from the envelope. It turned out to be a small handbill advertising the original contest which Jupiter had won.

It said:

WIN THE USE OF A ROLLS-ROYCE
Yours Complete with Chauffeur
For 30 days of 24 hours each!

GUESS THE NUMBER OF BEANS IN THE JAR
Rent-'n-Ride Auto Rental Agency

"Humph!" Mr. Gelbert said, looking at it. "What are you getting at? You had the use of the car for thirty days, any day you wanted, and every day has twenty-four hours, so that's that."

"I want you to study the wording of your advertisement again, sir," Jupiter said. "It says that the winner gets the use of the car for thirty days *of twenty-four hours each*."

"All right," Mr. Gelbert snapped. "You had it for thirty days and every day has twenty-four hours in it. Everybody knows that."

"Exactly, Mr. Gelbert," Jupiter Jones said. "Everyone knows a day has twenty-four hours in it, so why mention it at all? Why not just say, 'Win the use of a Rolls-Royce for thirty days'?"

"Why—uh—" Mr. Gelbert spluttered. "I was just trying to make it sound more, well, more splashy and interesting."

"Quite likely," Jupiter agreed, "but the way it reads to me is that the winner gets the use of the Rolls-Royce until he has used it for twenty-four hours thirty times. In other words, thirty days, each made up of twenty-four hours' *use* of the car. And according to my calculations—" he opened his notebook and studied what was written in it—"according to my calculations we have used the car for a total of seventy-seven hours and forty-five minutes, which is three days, five hours and forty-five minutes. So we have almost twenty-six days' use of the car left. Twenty-six days of twenty-four hours each, that is."

Pete and Bob could hardly believe their ears. It didn't seem possible Jupiter could be right, yet the way he explained it certainly sounded awfully plausible. After all, the contest had said, "thirty days of twenty-four hours each" and if each twenty-four hours' use made up one day, then—well, Jupe was right.

Mr. Gelbert seemed to have trouble speaking. He grew very red in the face.

"That's absurd!" he cried. "I never said anything like that. At least I didn't intend to say any such thing."

"That's why it's very important to always be careful you're saying what you mean," Jupiter replied. "In this case you did say—"

"I didn't!" Mr. Gelbert roared. "Anyway, if you think you can use my best car and driver free practically forever, you're crazy. I don't care what I said in the advertising. I meant thirty days, period. Your use of the car is finished! Period again!"

"But we were away for a week, Mr. Gelbert," Bob spoke up. "So we couldn't use the car. Couldn't we have that time added on to the thirty days, at least?"

"No!" the man started to shout automatically. Then he nodded abruptly. "All right, I'll make a concession. Providing you promise not to bother me any more, you can use the car two more times. That's two more times and after that—out!"

Jupiter sighed. He hated to have one of his schemes go wrong, and he had been counting on the wording in the advertising of the contest to win them the use of the car for some time to come. After all, what he had told Mr. Gelbert was perfectly logical. When you said "thirty days of twenty-four hours each," you meant thirty times twenty-four hours' use of the car. But adults, of course, were frequently neither reasonable nor logical.

"All right," he said. "Two more uses of the car. One of them at nine-thirty tomorrow morning. Thank you, Mr. Gelbert." He turned to his friends. "Come on, Second and Records."

Pete and Bob followed him out in silence, and they started back for the salvage yard.

"Gosh!" Pete said gloomily. "What are we going to do after we've finished the two times' use of the car? If we get any more mysteries to solve, we can't get around southern California on bicycles!"

"We'll have to work harder in the yard," Jupiter said, "so Aunt Mathilda won't mind letting us use the light truck, with Hans or Konrad to drive it."

"But half the time they're busy or the truck is away," Bob said. "This just about sinks The Three Investigators, Jupe. You know it does."

"We still can use the car twice more," Jupiter said firmly. "Something may turn up. I'm very much looking forward to our meeting tomorrow with Hector Sebastian. I have a feeling he has a real mystery for us to work on."

THE MYSTERIOUS MESSAGE _____ 3

"GUYS," said Hector Sebastian, "I want you to meet a young English friend of mine. His name is August. In fact, it's August August, which makes it unique. August, I'd like you to meet Jupiter Jones, Pete Crenshaw, and Bob Andrews. They've solved a number of baffling mysteries, and they may be able to help you."

The Three Investigators were seated in August's hotel room in the Hotel Imperial. The boy who now rose from a chair beside Mr. Sebastian was tall and thin—taller than Pete, and much thinner, with very light hair cut rather long. He wore horn-rimmed glasses, which seemed to perch on top of his thin, high-bridged nose.

"I'm terribly glad to meet you chaps," August August said as he strode over to shake their hands. "Please call me Gus."

He sat down again, and went on, "I certainly hope that you can help me because I'm stumped—

that's what you Americans say, isn't it? My great-uncle, Horatio August, recently died, and his lawyer sent me a paper that—well, I can't make head nor tail of it."

"Neither can I," Mr. Sebastian confessed. "Yet Horatio August seemed to think his great-nephew could unravel it. August, why don't you show the boys the letter?"

Gus took a wallet from his pocket and carefully removed from it a folded sheet of fine paper. It was covered with lines of spidery handwriting.

"Here," he said, handing it to Jupiter. "See what it means to you."

Bob and Pete crowded close to Jupiter and read the writing over his shoulder. It said:

To August August, my great-nephew:

August is your name and August is your fame and in August is your fortune. Let not the mountain of difficulty in your way stop you; the shadow of your birth marks both a beginning and an ending.

Delve deeply; the meaning of my words is for you alone. I dare not speak more plainly lest others find what is meant for you. It is mine; I paid for it and I own it, yet I have not dared its malevolence.

But fifty years have passed and in half a century

it should have purified itself. Yet still it must not be seized or stolen; it must be bought, given, or found.

Therefore take care, though time is of the essence. This and all my love I leave you.

Horatio August

"Wow!" Bob said. "That's some letter."

"It's all Greek to me," Pete said. "What does 'malevolence' mean?"

"It means—well, that somebody or maybe something would like to hurt you," Bob said.

Jupiter held the paper to the light to see if he could find any secret message on it.

"I had the same idea, Jupe," Mr. Sebastian said. "Unfortunately there is no secret writing, no invisible ink, or anything like that on the paper. I had it tested by a friend of mine who's a technical expert. The lawyer who sent it to August says that he saw Mr. August write it a few days before his death. Mr. August handed it to the lawyer right away with instructions to forward it when he died. So the message it holds is contained in the written words. What do you think?"

"Well . . ." Jupiter spoke cautiously, ". . . in one way it is very clear."

"Very clear!" Pete snorted. "I like that! To me it seems as clear as a Pacific fog at midnight!"

Jupiter didn't seem to hear him. He was concentrating on the strange message.

"For one thing," he observed, "it is clear that Mr. August wanted to send his grand-nephew a message no one else would understand. He's hidden something, and it sounds as if it's been hidden for fifty years. It's something valuable, so other people might steal it if he just came right out and told his great-nephew where it was. All of that is clear enough."

"Well . . . yes," Pete agreed. "But the rest of it, that's clear as mud."

"It's possible," Jupiter continued, "that some of the words mean something, and the others are thrown in to put people off the track. Let's start at the beginning. 'August is your name.' "

"That's perfectly true," the English boy said seriously. "And I suppose you could say that August is my fame, too. I mean, being called August August brought me a lot of ribbing from the other fellows at school. I was the best-known boy in school for that reason."

"But what about 'in August is your fortune'?" Bob put in.

"That's a little puzzling," Jupiter admitted. "If he meant Gus would find his fortune in August, shouldn't he have said 'in August will be your fortune'? But he said the fortune *is* in August."

"That's right," Mr. Sebastian said. "Unless he made a mistake because he was writing fast."

The First Investigator shook his head. "No," he said, "this message reads to me as if it had been carefully thought out. I don't think we can guess yet what he meant by 'in August is your fortune.' "

"My birthday is in August," Gus said. "Two days from now. August sixth. That's why my father gave me August for a first name. He said at the time, 'An August in August can only be August.' Could my birthday have something to do with it? He does mention my birth in the next sentence."

Jupiter turned this over in his mind.

"I don't know," he said at last. "If your birthday is only two days off, perhaps that's why the message says 'time is of the essence.' "

"If we only have two days to solve the message, we're sunk," Pete said. "Two years would be more like it."

"Give Jupe a chance," Bob told him. "He's only started."

The First Investigator studied the letter again intently.

"The second sentence," he said. "It starts, 'Let not the mountain of difficulty stop you; the shadow of your birth marks both a beginning and an ending.' The first half of the sentence seems to be saying don't give up, but what the second half means, I haven't any idea."

"Actually, there was a shadow over my birth," Gus

said. "You see, my mother died when I was born. And so my birth was both a beginning and an ending—a beginning for my life, an ending for hers. That might be what Great-Uncle Horatio was referring to."

"Maybe," Jupiter said. "But I don't see how it fits. The next sentence, though, seems clear enough. 'Delve deeply; the meaning of my words is for you alone.' That says the message is just for you and not to give up without trying hard. The next sentence explains why. 'I dare not speak more plainly lest others find what is meant for you.' No mystery about that line."

"Right," commented Mr. Sebastian. "But what do you make of the next sentence: 'It is mine; I paid for it and I own it, yet I have not dared its malevolence'?"

"He's saying that whatever it is, he owns it legally and has a right to give it to August," Jupiter answered. "At the same time, he's saying he's afraid of it for some reason."

Then he read aloud, " 'But fifty years have passed and in half a century it should have purified itself. Yet still it must not be seized or stolen; it must be bought, given, or found.' " He looked at Pete and Bob.

"Analyze that part of the message, Second and Records," he said. "You need practice in this sort of thing."

"I guess he's saying he's owned whatever it is for fifty years," Pete said. "And he thinks it has purified itself, meaning it won't hurt people any more."

"But it can still be dangerous," Bob added. "Or he wouldn't say, 'Yet still it must not be seized or stolen; it must be bought, found or given.' Then at the end he says, 'Therefore take care,' meaning to be careful how you handle whatever-it-is, I suppose. And he adds, 'Time is of the essence,' meaning time is very important, so you have to hurry even while you're being careful."

"The final line, 'This and all my love I leave to you,' is straightforward," Jupiter concluded. "Which brings us to the end of the mysterious message, knowing only a little more than when we started."

"You can say that again!" Pete exclaimed.

"I think we ought to know more about Horatio August. What was your great-uncle like, Gus?"

"I don't know," the English boy said. "I never saw him in my life. He was a mystery man of the family. As a boy, long before I was born, he sailed away on a trading ship for the South Seas. The family received a few letters from him, then he dropped out of sight. We assumed he'd been on a ship that had sunk. It was a great surprise to me and to my father to receive the letter from the lawyer, saying Uncle Horatio had been living here in Hollywood but was dead now and had left instructions to send me the message."

"And you came here from England as soon as you got the message?" Jupiter asked.

"As soon as I could," Gus told him. "That wasn't immediately. I didn't get out of school till mid-July and then I had to wait for an opening on a charter flight to America. Actually, I got the message almost two months ago."

"As soon as you got here, I suppose you went to the lawyer who sent you the message?"

Gus shook his head.

"I telephoned him but he was out of the city, so I couldn't see him right away. I don't know a soul in America. But my father knows Mr. Sebastian well, so I rang him up. It was Mr. Sebastian who suggested telephoning you, of course. You fellows and Mr. Sebastian are the only ones I've spoken to so far."

"In that case," Jupiter said, "I think we should go with you to call on the lawyer, and learn all we can about your great-uncle. That will help us decide our next move."

"A terrific idea, Jupe," Mr. Sebastian said. "August, you can certainly trust The Three Investigators. Unfortunately, I have to get back to work now, so I'll leave you in their capable hands."

The Rolls-Royce was waiting outside, an ancient, boxlike automobile of majestic appearance, its body gleaming black, all its metal parts gold-plated.

Worthington, the tall, erect English chauffeur, held the door for them to enter.

Gus took out a folded letter which contained the lawyer's name—H. Dwiggins—and an address in an older part of town. A moment later they were driving through the streets of Hollywood. Gus kept the boys busy with questions about the movie capital until, a few minutes later, Worthington nosed the Rolls-Royce into a narrow driveway that led up to a rather small, old-fashioned stucco house.

"Hmm," Jupiter murmured as they climbed out of the car. "Mr. Dwiggins apparently has his office in his home."

A small card over the doorbell said *H. Dwiggins— Attorney-at-Law—Ring and Walk In.*

Jupiter pressed the doorbell and they could hear a faraway ring. Then, obeying the instructions on the card, he opened the door.

They found themselves in a living room that had been turned into an office. It held a big desk, many shelves of law books, and several filing cabinets. One filing cabinet stood open, a folder of papers was scattered on the desk, and a wooden swivel chair lay toppled on its side. But Mr. Dwiggins was nowhere to be seen.

"Something's happened here!" Jupiter exclaimed. "There's something wrong." He raised his voice. "Mr. Dwiggins! Mr. Dwiggins! Are you here?"

They waited breathlessly in the silence that followed.

Then a muffled voice, very faint and far away, answered them.

"Help!" it cried. "Help! I'm suffocating."

CRY FOR HELP

"HELP ME!" the muffled voice came again. "I'm smothering."

"There!" Pete pointed to a closet door in the opposite wall, between two sets of bookshelves. It had a spring lock on the outside, the kind that locked automatically. Pete turned it, pulled, and the door swung open.

A small man was sitting on the floor of the closet, gasping for breath. His gold-rimmed glasses hung from one ear, his tie was twisted to one side, and his white hair was rumpled.

"Thank goodness you came," he whispered. "Please help me up."

Bob and Pete crowded into the small closet to help him to his feet, and Jupiter picked up the overturned swivel chair. As he set it upright, an expression of surprise crossed his face.

"Very odd," he said under his breath.

The boys helped Mr. Dwiggins to the chair, and

he drew a deep breath. His hands shaking, he straightened his tie and put his glasses on properly.

"You came just in time," he said. "A little longer in there and I might have suffocated." Then, getting a good look at them, he blinked.

"But who are you?" he asked. "You're just boys!"

"I'm August August, sir," the English boy said. "You told me to call on you today."

"Oh yes." Mr. Dwiggins nodded. "And these are friends of yours?"

"This will help explain, sir," Jupiter answered and produced from his pocket a printed card which he handed to the lawyer. It said:

THE THREE INVESTIGATORS
"We Investigate Anything"

? ? ?

First Investigator . . . . Jupiter Jones
Second Investigator . . . Peter Crenshaw
Records and Research . . . Bob Andrews

"You're investigators?" the lawyer seemed surprised.

"They're going to help me solve the mysterious message Great-Uncle Horatio sent me, sir," Gus said.

"Oh." Mr. Dwiggins blinked again. He peered once

more at the card. "It's a very impressive card, young man. But may I ask what the question marks stand for?"

The three had been waiting for that question. Hardly anyone failed to ask it when they saw the card.

"The question mark, otherwise known as the interrogation mark," Jupiter said, "stands for things unknown, questions unanswered, mysteries unsolved, riddles of any sort. Our business is answering the questions, unraveling the riddles, solving any mysteries which come our way. Hence, the question mark is the symbol of The Three Investigators."

"I see, I see," the lawyer murmured. "That's rather an ambitious program. Still, I like to see young people with self-confidence . . . But good gracious, I'm forgetting about my attacker!"

He sprang to his feet and looked around. He spotted the open filing cabinet.

"My confidential files! The scoundrel has been in my files! Now what did he take? What's this folder on my desk? I didn't leave it there!"

He snatched up the manila folder on the desk and began to leaf through the many papers inside.

"It's your great-uncle's folder!" he exclaimed to Gus. "I was his lawyer for twenty years and I kept all the papers relating to thc business I handled for him in here. Now why should anyone be interested in . . . the message! It's gone!"

He looked at Gus. "The fellow who attacked me took the copy I made of your great-uncle's message to you!" he exclaimed. "Although it seemed meaningless to me, your great-uncle obviously considered it very important, so I made a copy in case the original somehow was lost. Naturally, I expected it to be safe in my confidential files. But it's been stolen!"

"Please tell us just what happened, sir," Jupiter requested. "This new development may be very significant."

The lawyer put the file folder back in the cabinet and locked the drawer. Then he sat down and told them what he could.

Mr. Dwiggins had been seated at his desk, working on some papers, when the door had opened. He looked up to see a man of average height, with a black moustache and heavy eyeglasses. As Mr. Dwiggins was about to speak, the intruder reached out and put a hand over his eyes, half knocking off his glasses. Before the lawyer could make any move to defend himself, his attacker had pulled him from his chair, dragged him across the room, and closed him in the coat closet, which automatically locked.

At first Mr. Dwiggins had hammered on the locked door, shouting for help. However, as he lived alone there was no one to hear him except the man who had locked him in. Realizing this, Mr. Dwiggins had stopped shouting and listened.

After a few minutes, he heard the outer door open and shut, indicating his attacker had left. Again he hammered on the closet door and shouted, until he realized he was only using up precious oxygen.

"Then I sat down on the floor and waited for help," Mr. Dwiggins finished. "I knew the air in the closet would only last a few hours. Thank goodness you came when you did!"

"What time did this happen, sir?" Jupiter asked.

"I'm not sure," Mr. Dwiggins answered. "Let's see, it's now—" He looked at his wristwatch. The hands had stopped at 9:17, more than an hour and a half before.

"My watch!" he exclaimed. "It must have broken when that scoundrel threw me into the closet."

"That means whoever it was has had nearly two hours to get away," Jupiter said. "He could be anywhere now. Did you notice anything else about him, Mr. Dwiggins? Anything that might be a clue?"

"I'm sorry. I was so surprised I just had time to notice his moustache and glasses and the way his eyes seemed to gleam behind the lenses."

"Not much help there," Pete put in.

"I guess not," Jupiter agreed. "Do you see anything else in here that could have been disturbed, Mr. Dwiggins?"

The lawyer looked around his office.

"Apparently he went straight to the filing cabinet,"

he said. "Then as soon as he found what he wanted, he left."

"Hmmm," Jupiter murmured. "That means he knew exactly what he was looking for, and of course he could find the right file because the folders are arranged alphabetically. But how did he know about the message in the first place?"

Mr. Dwiggins blinked. "Why—I don't know."

"Was there anyone else around when Mr. August wrote the message?" Jupiter asked.

Mr. Dwiggins nodded. "Yes," he said. "The couple who took care of him. An old fellow and his wife. They'd been with him for years. She did the housekeeping and he tended the lawn and the garden. Name's Jackson. But when he died they went to San Francisco. Still, they were both of them in and out. One of them could have heard Mr. August telling me the message was vitally important and I must get it to his great-nephew without fail the moment he died."

"They could have told somebody else about it," Pete suggested. "This somebody could have guessed Mr. Dwiggins would make a copy, and come here to look."

"Mr. August was generally supposed to have a lot of money hidden somewhere," the lawyer said. "Anyone hearing of a secret message would instantly jump to the conclusion that it told where to find the money. Actually, though, Mr. August died in rather poor circumstances. His home was mortgaged and the mortgage holder is taking possession of it. I had to have the furnishings sold to pay his final bills."

"But the message indicates that he hid something valuable for me to find," Gus said. "Something he was afraid of for some reason."

"Yes, that's true." Mr. Dwiggins took off his glasses and wiped them. "Whatever it was, he kept it a secret from me. Several times he said to me, 'Henry, there are things about me you're better off not knowing. One of them is my right name, which isn't Harry Weston. Another is—but never mind. Just remember this: if you ever see a dark-skinned man with three dots tattooed on his forehead hanging around here, look out for stormy weather.'

"A very strange man, Mr. Weston—I mean, Mr. August. Strange but likable. Naturally, I never tried to pry into his secret, whatever it was."

"Excuse me, sir!" Jupiter Jones blurted out. "Do I understand that Mr. August was actually known as Mr. Weston?"

"Why yes. All the time he lived in Hollywood he called himself Harry Weston. It was only when he was near death and gave me his great-nephew's name and address that he revealed his true name to me."

Jupiter's gaze turned toward the filing cabinet drawer which they had seen open when they first entered. On the front was lettered *A-C*.

"Excuse me, Mr. Dwiggins," Jupiter said, "but I notice you put the file folder in the *A* drawer—*A* for *August,* of course. I suppose that when you learned his real name you changed the name on the folder from Weston to August?"

"Yes, of course. I do like to be accurate in these matters."

"But apparently the man who attacked you knew right where to look for it," Jupiter persisted. "Why didn't he look under *Weston* in the *W* file?"

"Why, I don't know." Mr. Dwiggins pondered. "Unless the Jacksons heard him tell me his real name . . . Oh, of course. I have something to show you."

He went to the *A* file and brought out a slip of paper. It was a clipping from a newspaper.

"This was in the Los Angeles paper," the lawyer said. "A reporter got wind of the fact that there was some mystery about Mr. Weston. He came pestering me and as Mr. August was dead, I saw no harm in telling his real name and what little else I knew about him. It's all there, so anyone could have read it."

The other three crowded around Jupiter to see the newspaper clipping. The small headline said: MAN OF MYSTERY DIES AT SECLUDED HOME IN LONELY DIAL CANYON.

Jupiter read the newspaper article rapidly. From it he learned that Mr. Horatio August, using the name of Harry Weston, had come to Hollywood about twenty years before, after living for many years in the West Indies. He apparently then had a good deal of money, earned as a young man in trading ventures in the South Seas and the Orient.

He had purchased a large house in Dial Canyon, in the remote hills north of Hollywood, and had lived there very quietly with only two servants to attend him. Making no friends, he had contented himself with collecting old clocks and books, especially old Latin books. He had also collected as many different editions as he could of the works of Sir Arthur Conan Doyle. As a boy in England he had once met the famous author, and was a great admirer of his fictional detective, Sherlock Holmes.

He had lived quietly under his assumed name until his death, after a brief illness for which he had refused to go to the hospital. He had said that one of his ambitions had been to die quietly in his own bed, and he proposed to do so now.

A tall man, with bushy white hair, he had never allowed himself to be photographed. His only known relatives lived in England. After his death the doctor who signed his death certificate had found upon his body the scars of many old wounds, apparently inflicted by a knife during some untold adventure of his youth.

Nothing else could be learned about his mysterious past.

"Boy!" Pete breathed. "He certainly was a man of mystery."

"Knife scars!" Gus said. "He must have had a very adventurous life. I wonder if he could have been a smuggler."

"He was hiding from someone," Bob chimed in. "That's pretty plain. First he must have hidden in the West Indies, then apparently he got scared he'd be found, and came here to hide in Dial Canyon. I guess he figured there are so many strange people in Los Angeles and Hollywood that he wouldn't create any stir here."

"Anyway," Jupiter added, "he did die quietly in bed. But if that was his ambition, it means he was afraid of violence from someone, presumably someone with a dark complexion and three dots tattooed on his forehead."

"Wait a moment!" Gus cried. "I'm just remembering—something happened about ten years ago when I was very small . . ." He frowned in an effort to remember.

"One night after I'd gone to bed, I heard voices downstairs—my father talking to someone. Then I heard Father raise his voice. He said, 'I tell you I don't know where my uncle is! As far as we know, he died long ago. If he is alive, I couldn't tell you where he is, not even for a million pounds.'

"That aroused me and I got out of bed and went to

the head of the stairs. My father and a strange man were standing in the middle of the living room. The stranger said something I couldn't hear, and my father answered, 'I don't care how important it is to you. I never heard of The Fiery Eye. And I've never heard from my uncle. Now get out and leave me alone!'

"When Father said that, the tall man bowed and turned to pick up his hat. He looked up and saw me, but he acted as if I wasn't there. He took his hat, bowed again, and went out. Father never mentioned the visitor, and I didn't ask about it because I knew he'd be angry at my listening when I was supposed to be in bed. But—"

Gus lowered his voice. "The man who'd been talking to Father had a dark complexion, and three dark spots on his forehead. I couldn't figure out what they were at the time. Now I realize they must have been small tattoo marks."

"Wow!" Bob said. "Three-Dots was trying to locate your great-uncle through your father."

"Which is why Great-Uncle Horatio never communicated with us, I expect," Gus said. "He didn't want to be located."

"The Fiery Eye," Jupiter murmured. "Mr. Dwiggins, did Mr. August ever mention such a thing to you?"

"No, my boy. I knew him for twenty years and he never mentioned it. All that I know about him is in that newspaper article. I regret now that I gave the reporter the information, but there seemed no harm in it at the time. One thing I must add—toward the end he became very secretive. Seemed to feel there were enemies around and he was being spied upon. Didn't even trust me. So he might easily have hidden something to keep it out of the hands of these imaginary enemies, and then sent you the message that he thought would enable you to locate it."

"I see," Jupiter said. "Well, we came to ask you about Mr. August, and I guess we've learned everything we can from reading the article. I think our next move is to visit the house in Dial Canyon and see if we can learn anything there."

"There's nothing there now but the empty house," Mr. Dwiggins told him. "As Mr. August's executor, I sold off all the books and furnishings to pay his debts. In three or four days the gentleman who owns the mortgage on the house is going to tear it down and erect modern homes on the land.

"If you want to visit the empty house, you may—I can give you permission, and a key to let you in. However, I don't know what you can find, because it's quite empty. There were a few books left, up till yesterday. And of course the statues—busts, that is. Plaster heads of famous men. However, they weren't worth anything so I sold them all to a junk dealer for a few dollars—"

"Busts!" Jupiter moved as if he had been stung by a bee. Plaster busts from an old house! Why, those must be the ones Titus Jones had brought to the salvage yard the day before. Caesar, Washington, Lincoln, and the rest.

"Mr. Dwiggins," Jupiter said swiftly, "we have to go now. Thank you very much. I think I understand the meaning of the secret message. But we have to hurry."

He turned and walked quickly out. Perplexed, Bob, Pete, and Gus followed. The Rolls-Royce was waiting, with Worthington polishing its shiny blackness with loving care.

"Worthington," Jupiter ordered as they all piled into the car, "back home! We have to hurry!"

"Very good, Master Jones," the chauffeur agreed. He backed the car out of the driveway, and headed for Rocky Beach at the fastest legal limit of speed.

"Gosh, Jupe, what's the rush?" Pete asked. "You act as if we were going to a fire!"

"Not a fire," Jupiter said mysteriously. "A Fiery Eye."

"I don't get you." Pete scowled. Bob, however, thought he understood.

"Jupe," he cried, "you've solved the secret message! Is that it?"

Jupiter nodded, trying to hide his look of satisfaction.

Gus gaped at him. "You really mean it?" he asked.

"I think I have," Jupiter replied. "The answer lies in your great-uncle's admiration for the stories about Sherlock Holmes, and in the plaster busts which Mr. Dwiggins mentioned."

"I don't get it," Pete groaned. "Sherlock Holmes—plaster busts—do they have a connection with the message?"

"I'll explain in more detail later," Jupiter said. "For the moment, please recall that one line of the message tells Gus that 'In August is your fortune.'"

"Well?" Pete looked blank. So did Gus. Bob, however, followed Jupiter's thinking.

"Those plaster busts of famous people," he said. "Washington, Lincoln, and so on. And one of them was the head of Augustus of Poland."

"'In August is your fortune'!" Gus said excitedly. "August—Augustus! You mean something is hidden inside the plaster bust of Augustus?"

"I'm practically sure of it," Jupiter replied. "It all fits together perfectly. Mr. August liked to read Sherlock Holmes stories for recreation. There's one called *The Adventure of the Six Napoleons* in which a valuable object is hidden in a bust of Napoleon. That must have given Mr. August an idea for hiding this Fiery Eye where no one would suspect it—in an ordinary plaster bust. He chose Augustus because the name was so much like his own, and Gus's here, that he was sure Gus or his father would figure it out. Notice that the words 'In August is' sound like 'in Augustus.'

"We'll know in a few moments. Of course, we will have to pay Aunt Mathilda five dollars for the bust so we can break it open, but luckily she owes us some money for repairing that washing machine and the lawnmower Uncle Titus bought last week."

The other three broke into a clamor of excited conversation, which continued until Worthington turned into the main gate of The Jones Salvage Yard. He had hardly brought the car to a stop before all four were out and streaking toward the office.

A few steps from the little cabin, Jupiter stopped so suddenly that the others bumped into him and all four fell down in a tangle of arms and legs. Then they saw what had made him stop.

On the table where thirteen plaster busts had stood early that morning, there now stood only five. They were Washington, Franklin, Lincoln, Francis Bacon, and Theodore Roosevelt.

The bust of Augustus of Poland was gone!

THREE-DOTS APPEARS __ 5

S L O W L Y the boys got to their feet, staring at the five busts that remained. Above them a hand-lettered sign had been tacked to the wall of the office: UNUSUAL GARDEN ORNAMENTS . . . ONLY $5.

Disappointment kept the boys silent for a few moments. At last Jupiter swallowed hard and called to his aunt who was sitting at a desk inside the small cabin.

"Aunt Mathilda! Where are the other busts?"

"Where are they?" Mathilda Jones came outside. "Why, I sold them, of course. This is Saturday and every Saturday morning lots of people wander through looking for something unusual to buy, as you know perfectly well, Jupiter."

Jupe nodded slowly. The reputation of The Jones Salvage Yard as a place where one might find almost anything brought buyers from all over.

"Well," Mathilda Jones went on, "I knew that few people would want old statues like those in their new, modern houses. But set out on a pedestal in the garden, they'd be something unique. The idea caught on fine. I sold eight of them for five dollars apiece. We already have a profit over what Titus paid for them."

"I don't suppose—" Jupiter's tone was not very hopeful—"I don't suppose you took the names and addresses of the buyers?"

"Mercy and goodness and sweetness and light, why should I do a thing like that? They just bought the statues and rode off with them."

"Can you tell us anything at all about the people who bought them? Especially Augustus of Poland?"

"Now why in the world are you suddenly interested in those old statues?" Mrs. Jones demanded. "Two of them were bought by a man in a black station wagon. I think he lives in North Hollywood. Two were bought by a lady in a red sedan. She's from Malibu, she said. The other four I didn't notice much, I was too busy."

"I see. Well—" Jupiter sighed. "I guess that's that. Come on, fellows, we'd better have a conference."

He led the way toward his workshop section. Gus's eyes were wide as Jupiter removed the iron grating that hid the entrance to Tunnel Two, and led them all through the big corrugated pipe into Headquarters.

When Gus had been shown the tiny laboratory, the little photographic darkroom, the See-All periscope Jupe had installed so they could see over the piles of junk that hid the trailer from the world, and their other special equipment, they settled themselves in the miniature office.

"Well?" Pete said. "Now what? If Mr. Augustus held Gus's fortune, whatever it is, he's gone. He's standing in somebody's garden and the only way we can find him is to find the garden. Since there are only about a hundred thousand gardens in this region, we might find the right one by the time we're ninety."

"It was a good try," Gus spoke up, trying to hide his disappointment. "You fellows couldn't know those busts were important when Mr. Jones bought them. But I'm afraid Augustus is gone for good now. I suppose that's what Great-Uncle Horatio meant when he said that time was of the essence. He was afraid something would happen to the busts if I didn't hurry and —well, it has."

"Perhaps the busts are lost to us beyond recall," Jupiter said at last. "But I do not intend to concede defeat yet. We are investigators. We'll just have to keep investigating."

"How?" Bob wanted to know.

"I don't know yet," Jupiter said. "I am giving the matter thought."

"I've got it!" Bob yelled. "We can try a Ghost-to-Ghost Hookup!"

"Ghost-to-Ghost Hookup?" Gus blinked in bewilderment. "Do you have direct contact with the other world for information?"

"Not quite." Bob grinned. "But it's almost as good. Tell me, who notices things most in any neighborhood? I mean, things like strangers hanging around, a new car in some family, anything unusual?"

"Why—" Gus thought a moment—"I don't know."

"Kids, of course," Pete put in. "Nobody notices kids hanging around, but nothing that happens gets by them. If someone has a new cat or dog, or someone hurts himself, or almost anything else, some kid in the neighborhood is bound to know about it."

"The only problem," Bob went on, "is to get in touch with enough boys and girls all over the city to find out what they know. They're always glad to help; kids have a natural interest in any kind of mystery."

"But how can you get in touch with enough boys and girls to do any good?" Gus asked. "You'd need to have some on the lookout for you in every part of the city."

"That's where the Ghost-to-Ghost Hookup comes in," Pete chimed in. "It was Jupe's idea, and it's a honey. You see, we all have some friends who don't know each other. And they all have other friends, and so on. When we want to find out something, we each phone five friends and tell them what we need to know. In this case we'll tell them to phone back at this number if they know of anyone who has just bought a plaster bust for a garden ornament.

"But if they don't know of anyone, each of them calls five of his friends and repeats the message. Then each of them calls five, and each of them calls five— well, it spreads like wildfire across the whole city. Inside of an hour we have boys and girls all over the city keeping their eyes open for plaster busts used as garden ornaments. They don't have to see them; they might hear their parents mention that some friend has bought one, and so on. It's like having thousands of assistants helping find something."

"My word!" Gus exclaimed. "If each of you calls five friends that's fifteen, and if each of them calls five, that's seventy-five—then it goes to three hundred and something, then into the thousands." He gave a low whistle. "It's fabulous!"

"We call all these kids who are helping us *ghosts*," Bob said. "It's a code name that keeps anyone who overhears us from guessing what we're talking about."

"Are you going to start phoning now, Jupiter?" Gus asked.

"This is Saturday afternoon," Jupiter said. "Most kids will be outdoors now. The time to call is after dinner. And that means a wait of several hours—"

"Jupiter!" It was his aunt's voice, coming in the open skylight of Headquarters. "Jupiter, you rascal, where are you?"

Jupiter reached for a microphone on the desk. It was wired to a small loudspeaker in the office. He had arranged this method of answering when his aunt or uncle called him.

"I'm right here, Aunt Mathilda," he said. "Did you want me?"

"Stars and comets!" his aunt exclaimed. "I can't get used to you talking at me from that contraption. I wish I knew what you were up to, Jupiter. It must be something extra special or you wouldn't have forgotten about lunch."

Lunch! At the word all four boys remembered they were hungry. Until now they had been too excited to think of food.

"Yes, Aunt Mathilda," Jupiter said. "I guess we did forget. I hope you don't mind that we brought a friend with us."

"Lands," his aunt said, "what's an extra boy when I have three around all the time?" It was true that Bob and Pete ate at Jupiter's house about as often as they ate at home.

"I have a box of sandwiches and some cold drinks for all of you. You can eat them in the office. I have to go downtown for a few hours, and Titus is away, so you'll have to mind the office this afternoon, Jupiter, and take care of any sales."

"Yes, Aunt Mathilda. We'll be right there."

They made their way through Tunnel Two to the workshop section, then through the yard to the office. Inside the small cabin they found piles of sandwiches wrapped in waxed paper, and several bottles of orange pop and root beer.

"There you are, boys," Mathilda Jones said. "I'm going downtown in the small truck. Hans is driving me. Don't leave until I get back and don't miss any sales, Jupiter."

"I won't, Aunt Mathilda."

With that, Mrs. Jones sailed out.

Without further words, the boys began to devour the sandwiches. When they had finished two apiece, and a bottle of pop, they felt able to talk again.

"Jupe," Pete said, munching on a roast beef sandwich, "what do you think is in this bust we're looking for? I mean if anything is?"

"Gus heard his father mention a 'Fiery Eye,' " Jupiter said. "I think The Fiery Eye is hidden inside the bust of Augustus of Poland."

"But what *is* The Fiery Eye?" Bob asked.

"It is something small," Jupiter said, "or it couldn't be hidden inside a plaster bust. Considering the care with which Gus's great-uncle hid it, and the fact that only fabulous jewels are given names, such as the Grand Mogul, Star of India, and Pasha of Egypt, it is my deduction that The Fiery Eye is a jewel which Mr. August brought from the Far East with him many years ago, and which is the reason he spent his life in hiding thereafter."

"Wow!" Pete breathed. "If you're right—"

"Sssh!" Bob hissed. "Here comes a customer."

A sleek sedan had pulled into the salvage yard and stopped just outside the office door. It was driven by a man in a chauffeur's uniform. The passenger, a tall, thin man, got out and stood for a moment looking at the five busts that remained on the bench beside the door.

Over his left arm hung a cane of polished black wood. With this he poked one of the busts lightly, then ran his fingers casually over the top of the plaster heads. Seeming unsatisfied, he wiped dust from his fingers and turned to the door of the office.

Jupiter was standing there waiting. The others, seated inside, could see past him. An unspoken excitement ran through them all.

The tall, thin customer was immaculately dressed, had a dark complexion, and jet black hair streaked with grey. Most important, on his forehead were three small dots.

"I beg your pardon," Three-Dots said, in excellent English. "These interesting statuettes—"

He pointed with his cane at the five busts. Jupiter blinked. He had seen the three dots before the others and reacted automatically. He let his body slump, his face droop, his eyes half close. Jupiter, stocky enough to be called fat by his enemies, could indeed look fat when he wanted to.

"Yes, sir?" Jupiter said. He spoke through his nose,

and to anyone who did not know him, looked and sounded like a fat moron.

"Have you any others?" Three-Dots' voice was cold and distant.

"Any others?" Jupe sounded as if he couldn't understand plain English.

"Yes, any others," Three-Dots repeated. "If you have, I would like to inspect them. I want something a little more unusual than George Washington or Benjamin Franklin."

"That's all there are," Jupiter said. "Others have been sold."

"Then there were others?" A flicker of interest lighted the deep-set, black eyes. "Their names, my boy?"

"I don't know." Jupiter closed his eyes as if trying to think. "Funny names. Like Homer Somebody. And Augustus of someplace."

"Why is he telling that?" Pete risked a low whisper to Bob.

"Jupe always has a reason," Bob whispered back. "Listen."

"Augustus!" Three-Dots' impassive face seemed alive for a moment. "Yes, I believe I would like a bust of Augustus. For my garden. You say it has been sold?"

"Yesterday," Jupe said.

"The name and address of the purchaser?" Three-

Dots' voice sounded as if he were giving Jupiter an order now. "I will buy it from him."

"We don't keep any records," Jupiter said. "It could have been anybody."

"Could . . . have . . . been . . . anybody." Three-Dots' voice was cold again. "I see. Most unfortunate. If you had the name and address I would be glad to reward you for giving it to me. One hundred dollars."

"We don't keep any records," Jupe said again, stupidly. "Sometimes people bring things back. If they bring it back you could have it. You want to leave your name and address?"

"A smart idea." Three-Dots looked hard at Jupiter. "I will do that."

Slinging his cane over his left wrist, he drew a card from his pocket and penciled an address on it. He handed it to Jupiter.

"There," he said. "Be sure to phone me. If Augustus comes back, I will pay one hundred dollars for him. You will not fail to call me?"

"I'll try not to," Jupiter promised in a dull voice.

"Be sure you do not!" Three-Dots suddenly jabbed his cane down on the ground.

"A bit of paper," he said. "I believe in cleanliness."

He thrust the cane at Jupiter. Gus, Bob and Pete all swallowed gasps of alarm. The cane was a sword cane. On its glittering 12-inch blade was a scrap of paper that had been littering the ground.

The needle-sharp point of the sword stopped only inches from Jupiter's chest. Slowly Jupiter reached out and took the paper off it. With another abrupt movement Three-Dots withdrew his cane, and once more it was just a cane, the sword blade gone.

"You will hear from me again," he said sharply. "In the meantime, if Augustus returns, phone me."

He turned, got into his car, and was gone.

STRANGE DEDUCTIONS ———— 6

J U P E waited until the car was out the gate, then he turned. He was pale.

"There's somebody not to fool around with!" Pete exclaimed. "I thought he was going to stick you, Jupe."

"He was warning me," Jupiter said with a slight gulp. "He was letting me know it'll be too bad for anybody who tries any tricks on him."

"I think that's the same man who called on my father ten years ago," Gus spoke up. "I can't be sure, but he looks like the same one."

"He has the same three dots on his forehead," Bob said. "And he looks as if he came from the Far East, maybe someplace in India. The three dots could be the mark of some special religious group."

"Why'd you let him know there had been an Augustus of Poland bust in the bunch?" Pete asked. "That really stirred him up."

"He seemed to know about the busts," Jupiter

said, taking a swallow of root beer. "I wanted to see if Augustus meant anything to him. It did, all right. Possibly *he* stole the copy of the message from Mr. Dwiggins."

"He doesn't wear glasses and a black moustache," Gus objected.

"He could have hired someone to do it for him," Bob suggested. "Anyway, he certainly had some idea Augustus was important."

"He was fishing for information," Jupiter said. "So was I. I persuaded him to give me his name and address."

He put the card Three-Dots had given him on the desk. It said, in engraved script:

Rama Sidri Rhandur
Pleshiwar, India

Under it he had written in pencil the name and address of a motor hotel in Hollywood.

"India!" Pete exclaimed. "Bob was right! But if Three-Dots is from some fanatical group in India who wants to get The Fiery Eye, I vote we forget the whole thing. I read a book about Indian tribesmen who were out to get back some kind of holy relic. They'd just as soon cut you up as look at you. Why, the look in that fellow's eyes—"

"So far we're just guessing," Jupiter said. "Bob, it is now time to do some research."

"Sure," Bob agreed. "What kind?"

"In the library," the First Investigator told him. "See if you can find out anything about The Fiery Eye. Also look up Pleshiwar, India."

"Right," Bob said. "Suppose I report back after dinner. My family sort of expects me to eat dinner at home once in awhile."

"That will be time enough," Jupiter told him. "We will start the Ghost-to-Ghost Hookup going then."

"My word!" Gus said as Bob pedaled away. "I had no idea what I was letting you in for! Somebody attacks Mr. Dwiggins—Three-Dots comes here and threatens you, Jupiter—there is obviously a lot at stake and a great deal of peril. I haven't any right to endanger you. I think I had better just go home and forget about The Fiery Eye. You can stop hunting for Augustus, and if Three-Dots or Black Moustache find him, they can fight it out between them."

"Gus, that's mighty good thinking!" Pete exclaimed. "How about it, Jupe?"

But the expression on Jupe's face gave him the answer. Give Jupiter Jones a good mystery to solve and it was like handing a steak to a hungry bulldog—he wasn't going to give it up!

"We've only just started on this investigation,

Second," Jupiter said. "We've been wanting a mystery to tackle, so we can't give up a good one when it comes along. Anyway, there are certain curious facts I haven't figured out yet."

"There are? Such as what?" Pete asked.

"It is my deduction," the First Investigator said, "that Mr. Dwiggins locked himself in the closet."

"Locked himself in the closet?" Gus's voice was full of astonishment. "Why should he do a thing like that?"

"I don't know. That's part of the mystery."

"What makes you think he locked himself in, First?" Pete asked. "I mean, he was locked inside and he certainly looked as if he had been handled roughly."

"Superficial evidence meant to mislead us," Jupiter said. "Think about it, Second. Use your ability to reason. Mr. Dwiggins said he'd been in the closet for an hour and a half, didn't he?"

"Well—yes."

"During which time he pounded on the door and called for help. Now what would a man do first under such circumstances?"

"He'd put his glasses on straight!" Gus cried. "Or else, because it was dark, take them off and put them in his pocket. He wouldn't let them hang by one ear for an hour and a half!"

"I guess you're right, Gus." Pete scratched his head.

"Also he'd straighten his tie. You're right, Jupe, he fixed his tie and glasses to make us think he'd been attacked."

"Always analyze all the facts," Jupiter said. "I must admit, though, that Mr. Dwiggins was very convincing. I might not have thought of being suspicious except for one fact. Come over here behind the desk, both of you, and put your hands on the seat of this chair."

He stood up. Pete and Gus both touched the wooden seat of the swivel chair.

"Now touch the desk," Jupiter directed. "And tell me the difference between the two wooden surfaces."

Both touched the desk. Gus exclaimed, "The chair is warm because you were sitting in it. The desk top is cooler."

Jupiter nodded. "And when I picked up Mr. Dwiggins' chair back in his office, I noticed to my surprise that the seat of it was slightly warm, as if someone had been sitting in it up to a minute or so before. Then when I thought about the eyeglasses and necktie, I realized what must have happened.

"Mr. Dwiggins saw us drive up and get out of the car. He knocked over the chair, hurried into the closet, and disarranged his eyeglasses and tie. Then he sat down and began to shout for help. He probably hadn't been in the closet more than two or three minutes before we found him."

"Wow!" Pete exclaimed. "Why would he do all that?"

"To deceive us," Jupe answered. "To make us think his copy of the message had been stolen, when it hadn't."

"You mean there was no middle-sized man with eyeglasses and a black moustache?" Gus asked.

"I don't think so. I think Mr. Dwiggins made him up. My theory is that Three-Dots, Mr. Rama Rhandur from India, may have paid Mr. Dwiggins for his copy of the secret message, and Mr. Dwiggins thought of this scheme to make us think it had been stolen."

"It certainly sounds logical," Gus admitted. "That would explain how Mr. Rhandur came here, too. He solved the message enough to realize the importance of those busts."

"And he said he'll be back!" Pete exclaimed. "Maybe he'll bring some of his buddies with him next time. Suppose he doesn't believe we really don't know where Augustus of Poland is? I bet Mr. Rhandur could think up some fierce tortures to make people talk. Don't forget he carries a sword cane."

"You're letting your imagination run away with you, Second," Jupiter told him. "We have no reason to think Mr. Rhandur would ever torture anyone."

"There always has to be a first time," Pete muttered darkly.

Gus was about to say something when the phone rang. Jupiter answered it. "Jones Salvage Yard, Jupiter Jones speaking."

"This is Mrs. Peterson. I live in Malibu Beach," said a pleasant-sounding woman's voice. "I'm sorry, but I have a complaint. Yesterday I bought two plaster busts from you folks to use as garden ornaments."

"Yes, Mrs. Peterson?" Jupiter spoke with sudden interest.

"Well, they were very dusty and I put them out in the yard under the hose to wash them off. One of them started to crumble. An ear fell off and part of the nose. My husband tells me they're just made of plaster, and should be kept indoors. Outside, the weather would ruin them in no time. I really feel you should return my money, as you sold them to me for garden ornaments."

"I'm very sorry, Mrs. Peterson," Jupiter said politely. "I guess we didn't think about plaster being affected by water. We'll return your money. May I ask which busts you bought?"

"I'm not sure. They're out in the patio now. But I think one of them is Augustus somebody. I'll bring them back tomorrow."

"Excuse me, Mrs. Peterson!" Jupiter said, sitting

up straight at the words. "We'll come and pick them up to save you the trouble. If you'll give me the address, we'll be over sometime this afternoon or evening."

He wrote rapidly as Mrs. Peterson gave him her address, then hung up.

"We've located Augustus of Poland!" he said to Pete and Gus. "As soon as Hans comes back with the small truck we'll go pick him up."

"Great!" Pete said. Then he added, "I hope we get Augustus before Three-Dots gets us!"

BLACK MOUSTACHE ON THE SCENE ———— 7

MEANWHILE, Bob had reached the Rocky Beach Public Library, where he had a part-time job. As he walked in, Miss Bennett, the librarian, looked up.

"Why, hello, Bob," she said. "I didn't know this was your day to work."

"It isn't," Bob said. "I came to do some research."

"Oh, and I hoped you were here to help me." Miss Bennett laughed lightly. "It's been such a busy day. There are so many books to put back on the shelves. Could you spare us a little time, Bob?"

"Sure, Miss Bennett," Bob agreed.

Miss Bennett asked him first to mend the binding on some juvenile books. Bob took them into the back storage room and used strong plastic tape to secure the torn covers. When he had finished, Miss Bennett had a sizable stack of returned books to be put back on the shelves. He put these away one by one, and then the librarian called his attention to some books that had been left on one of the reading-room tables. Bob gathered them up. As he looked at the one on top, he almost jumped in surprise.

The title was *Famous Gems and Their Stories*. It was the very book he had come to the library to consult.

"Something wrong, Bob?" Miss Bennett asked.

Bob shook his head. "No, Miss Bennett." He brought the book to the main desk to show it to her. "It's just that I came to look up something in this book and I was surprised to find it here."

"Goodness!" Miss Bennett read the title. "That is a coincidence. This book hasn't been looked at for years and now it's needed twice in the same day."

Bob didn't think it was a coincidence.

"I don't suppose you remember who was reading this book, do you?" he asked.

"I don't believe I do. So many people in today, they're just a blur in my mind."

Bob's mind raced. Who would be the most likely person? He tried a shot in the dark.

"Could it have been a man with large horn-rimmed glasses and a black moustache?" he asked. "A man about medium height?"

"Why—" Miss Bennett frowned, thinking. "Yes, it was. Now that you describe him, I remember. He had a rather low, husky voice. However did you know?"

"I heard about him from someone," Bob said. "If

there isn't anything else you need me to do—"

Miss Bennett shook her head, and Bob hurried to the reading table. Black Moustache had been here! That meant he was also on the trail.

He settled down to look through the book. It was full of interesting information about the discovery and history of the world's most famous jewels. Finally, after letting himself be sidetracked into reading the curious history of the Hope diamond, which had apparently brought bad luck to many people, he found what he was looking for. One chapter was titled *The Fiery Eye*. He turned to it.

The Fiery Eye was a ruby as big as a pigeon's egg, of an intense crimson color. No one knew where or when it had been discovered, but it had been known in China, India and Tibet for many centuries. It had belonged to rajahs, emperors, queens, princes and wealthy merchants. It had been stolen many times, and some of its owners had been murdered for it. Other times the owner had been defeated in battle, had lost his fortune, or otherwise suffered calamity. At least fifteen men were known to have died because of it.

The Fiery Eye was shaped rather like an eye, and was very valuable. It was not as valuable as some other famous gems, however, because it was flawed— there was a hollow inside it which made it imperfect.

The chapter ended with these words:

There are gems which seem to be followed by ill fortune. Owner after owner suffers death or illness or other serious loss. Violence hovers about them and no owner is safe. The Hope diamond, which was believed to bring misfortune to its owners until it was given to the Smithsonian Institution in Washington, D.C., is one such. The Fiery Eye is another. Few of its owners failed to suffer misfortune, until at last it was given as a token of repentance by a maharajah of India to the Temple of Justice, in the remote mountain village of Pleshiwar, India.

In the Temple of Justice, sacred to a small but fanatical band of warlike mountain tribesmen, The Fiery Eye was mounted in the forehead of the temple deity. Local superstition held that it could detect sin. If someone accused of a crime was brought before it, and The Fiery Eye blazed with light, this was considered proof of guilt. If The Fiery Eye remained dim, this was proof of innocence.

The stone vanished mysteriously from the temple many years ago. Its present whereabouts is unknown, though the followers of the Temple of Justice made vigorous efforts to find it. It is rumored to have been sold by a temple official who had been guilty of misconduct and feared the gem would expose his guilt. Many suppose the ill-fated

gem to lie in some unmarked grave with the bones
of the man who bought or stole it. Others believe
it will yet reappear. One old legend says that when
The Fiery Eye has dwelt unseen and untouched
for fifty years, it will be purified and no longer
bring ill fortune, providing it is bought, found or
given, not seized or stolen.

Few collectors, however, would care to risk the
supposed curse on the stone even now, though the
fifty years is almost up.

"Wow!" Bob breathed to himself. The Fiery Eye
certainly seemed a ruby to stay away from. Even
though the fifty years might be up now—the book he
was reading had been printed several years earlier—
he didn't think he'd want to risk having anything to
do with the gem.

Thoughtfully he put the book away. Then he got
down an encyclopedia to look up Pleshiwar, India.
He found a brief paragraph. It just said that inhabi-
tants of Pleshiwar and the surrounding mountains
were generally tall and warlike, extremely ferocious
in battle, and never gave up seeking vengeance on
anyone who injured them.

This made Bob gulp again. He wrote down
the main facts about Pleshiwar, as well as about the
ruby, and sat thinking. Should he phone Jupe now
and tell him? He decided not to. It was nearly dinner

time, and besides, Jupe was not going to start the Ghost-to-Ghost Hookup until later.

Bob said good-bye to Miss Bennett and biked home. His mother was just getting dinner, and his father was reading and smoking his pipe. He greeted Bob.

"Hi, son," he said. "Why so thoughtful? You look as if you were trying to solve some very large problem. Are you boys looking for another lost parrot or something like that?"

"No, Dad," Bob said. "Right now we're looking for a missing bust of Augustus of Poland. Do you know who he was?"

"I'm afraid I don't. But speaking of Augustus reminds me, this is August. Do you know how the month of August got its name?"

Bob didn't. His father told him, and Bob jumped as if jabbed with a pin. He made a beeline for the telephone and dialed The Jones Salvage Yard. Mathilda Jones answered and Bob asked for Jupiter.

"I'm sorry, Bob," Mrs. Jones told him. "Jupiter and the others left half an hour ago in the light truck with Hans. They had to go to Malibu."

"I'll be right over and wait for him!" Bob blurted out. "Thank you."

He hung up, but before he could get out the door, his mother's voice brought him back.

"Robert! Dinner is ready. Now you come sit down and eat. Whatever harum-scarum project you're engaged in, it can wait until you've had dinner."

Reluctantly Bob sat down. This was something Jupe had to know! But he supposed it could wait another hour.

At that moment, Jupiter, Pete and Gus were riding through the Malibu Beach section in search of Mrs. Peterson's home. They finally stopped in front of a large, attractive stucco dwelling with a spreading, well-kept garden.

Jupiter led the way up a path and across a tiled patio to the door. He pressed the bell and after a moment the door opened.

"I'm Jupiter Jones from The Jones Salvage Yard," Jupe said to the pleasant-faced woman in a summer dress who opened the door. "I've come to take back the plaster busts we sold you."

"Oh yes. They're over here."

The woman led the way around a corner, and there were the two busts, one looking much the worse for wear. As Mrs. Peterson had said, Augustus of Poland had lost one ear and his nose, and the rest of him looked rather crumbly. The other, Francis Bacon, had not been washed and looked dusty but intact.

"I'm sorry to have to return them," the woman

said, "but they were sold for garden ornaments, and my husband says our sprinklers would wash them away in no time."

"That's perfectly all right, ma'am," Jupiter said, concealing his delight at getting Augustus back. "Here is your money—we'll take the busts away now."

He handed Mrs. Peterson ten dollars that his aunt had given him, then picked up Augustus and, grunting a little, carried the bust out to the truck. Pete followed with Francis Bacon. They laid the busts carefully on the front seat between Gus and Hans, and climbed on the back of the truck. Then they started back for Rocky Beach.

"Golly, do you suppose The Fiery Eye is in Augustus?" Pete asked Jupe excitedly as they rode.

"I consider there is an excellent chance," Jupe answered.

"As soon as we get back to the yard, we have to break him open," Pete said.

"We must wait for Records to return," Jupiter told him. "He'd be disappointed if we smashed Augustus without him."

At the salvage yard, Bob was sitting in the office with Mathilda Jones, waiting for the boys to return. On Saturdays the yard stayed open until fairly late, to allow people to come and browse around. Usually a fair number of people were engaged in inspecting

the many curious items The Jones Salvage Yard had
to offer. This evening, however, only a couple of men
were strolling around, looking at old tools and
machinery.

A black sedan drove up, and a man got out and
came to the door. Bob gulped at the sight of him.

He was a man of average height, with black hair,
horn-rimmed glasses and a large black moustache.

Black Moustache! Here!

"Good evening," Black Moustache said to Mathilda
Jones in a hoarse voice, "I'm interested in these
handsome and artistic busts you display here." He
turned to look at the five busts that still sat in a
row outside the office. "Mmmm—very famous people.
Do you have any others?"

"That's all there are," Mathilda Jones told him.
"And I can't sell them to you for garden ornaments.
I've just learned they dissolve if they get too wet. In
fact, two are being returned and I suppose the others
will be eventually."

She sounded upset. It always upset Mathilda Jones
to give back money. She was big-hearted and
generous, but she was also a business woman and
liked to make a profit out of the odd things Titus
Jones bought.

"Indeed?" Black Moustache sounded interested.
"Two are being returned and others may be. I am a
collector, and I will buy these five from you for the

price you have set—five dollars each. But you must promise to save for me any others that come back, for I want them all."

"You do?" Mathilda Jones brightened up at the words. "But some of them may be damaged when people try to wash them."

"That doesn't matter. If you will promise to save every single one for me, I'll buy these now as well as the two that you say are being returned."

"It's a deal," Mathilda Jones said. "Buy these and you'll get any that are returned. The two that are coming back should be here any minute. My nephew went to pick them up."

"Excellent!" Black Moustache brought out some bills. "Here is thirty-five dollars for these five and the two coming. Now, I will load these fine artistic busts into my car."

Bob was quivering with excitement, trying to think of some way to interrupt, and knowing he couldn't. Mrs. Jones had just finished a business deal and she prided herself that she never went back on her word. Jupiter was bringing back two busts, and maybe one of them was Augustus.

And Black Moustache could claim it because he had already paid for it!

"Bob, what in the world is the matter with you?" Mrs. Jones asked, eyeing him sharply. "You have the twitches tonight. Anything wrong?"

"I think——" Bob spoke with an effort——"I think our new friend Gus wanted one of those busts, Mrs. Jones. They came from his great-uncle's house and, well——"

"I'm sorry, you should have spoken sooner. They all belong to that gentleman now, and here comes the truck."

Black Moustache had just finished stowing the last of the five busts in his car as the truck rattled up and stopped.

Jupe and Pete jumped off the back of the truck and hurried around to the cab. Hans handed down the two plaster busts. Pete took Francis Bacon and Jupe took Augustus of Poland, clasping it tenderly to his chest.

Neither of them noticed Black Moustache until the man hurried over to them.

"Boys, those belong to me!" he snapped. He reached for the bust of Augustus in Jupe's arms and grabbed it firmly. "That's mine," he growled. "And I mean to have it. Now let go!"

BOB SPRINGS A SURPRISE

BLACK MOUSTACHE tugged. Jupiter pulled, unwilling to let go of Augustus. Black Moustache shouted at him angrily, "Let go, I tell you! This bust is mine. I bought it and paid for it!"

"Let him have it, Jupiter!" Mrs. Jones called sternly.

"But Aunt Mathilda!" Jupiter protested, clinging tightly to the plaster bust. "I promised our friend Gus this one."

"I'm sorry, but it's too late," Mrs. Jones said. "I've sold it to this gentleman."

"But it's vitally important to Gus!" Jupiter gasped. "It's practically a matter of life and death."

"Pooh, life and death because of an old plaster statue?" Mrs. Mathilda Jones snorted. "You boys have over-active imaginations. Now give the bust to that gentleman, Jupiter. The Jones Salvage Yard never goes back on a deal."

"Give it to me!" Black Moustache snarled. He gave

an extra-hard jerk just as Jupiter, obeying his aunt, let go. The man staggered backwards, tripped over a rock, and fell to the ground. The bust rolled out of his arms and cracked into a dozen pieces.

The boys stared at the pieces with mouths open.

Mrs. Jones was too far away to see, but Jupiter and Gus and Pete and Bob saw it plainly. A red stone the size of a pigeon's egg, shimmering in the center of the broken plaster head!

For a moment no one moved. Then Black Moustache scrambled to his feet, picked up the red stone and jammed it in his pocket.

He turned to Mrs. Jones. "Entirely my fault," he said. "I accept full responsibility. Now if you will excuse me, I must go. I won't want any more busts."

He leaped into his car and drove swiftly out of the salvage yard while the boys watched him go in despair.

"He's got it," Pete groaned. "He's got The Fiery Eye!" Then he remembered their earlier conversation. "But I thought we decided there wasn't any man with a black moustache. Mr. Dwiggins made him up."

"Obviously we were wrong in some way," Jupe said. His body slumped, his face drooped; he looked very depressed.

"Black Moustache was at the library earlier today," Bob put in. "He was looking up The Fiery Eye."

"This is an upsetting turn of events," Jupiter said

slowly. "We no sooner find The Fiery Eye than we lose it again. I'm sorry, Gus."

"It wasn't your fault," the English boy said stoutly. "Please don't blame yourself."

"I was so sure Black Moustache didn't exist—" Jupiter began. He was interrupted by his aunt.

"Well, Jupiter, I'm glad he took the blame," she said, nodding toward the lumps of plaster that had been Augustus of Poland. "It was his fault, actually, because he dropped it, but people aren't always reasonable. However, no harm done. Just clean up those pieces and put them in the trash barrel."

"Yes, Aunt Mathilda," Jupiter said.

Mrs. Jones looked at the clock over the door of her office. "Time to close up," she said. "Unless you boys want to stay here a while longer."

"We have something to talk about," Jupiter told her. "We'd like to stay a little longer."

"Then we'll leave the gate open," Mrs. Jones said. "No use missing a possible customer. You wait on anyone who comes."

Jupiter agreed, and Mrs. Jones left the yard for the small two-story house just outside the wall where she and Titus and Jupiter lived.

The four boys were left alone in The Jones Salvage Yard. They picked up the broken pieces of Augustus and carried them over to an old table. Jupiter examined them.

"See?" he said, pointing to an egg-shaped cavity in the broken pieces. "Here's where The Fiery Eye was."

"And now Black Moustache has it!" Bob groaned. "We'll never get it back again."

"It does seem rather hopeless," Jupiter agreed—and it was very rare for Jupiter to admit the possibility of defeat. "But let us explore the possibilities. Come back to our workshop and, Bob, you tell us what you found out."

He led the way back to the secluded workshop area. Settled beside the printing press and the lathe, the boys listened as Bob read from his notes all that he had learned about the blood-stained history of The Fiery Eye, and about the people of Pleshiwar, India.

"Golly!" Pete gulped. "I don't like the sound of all that! If The Fiery Eye is a bad luck ruby, I say let's leave it alone. Let it jinx somebody else."

"But part of the legend is that if The Fiery Eye goes unseen and untouched for fifty years, it will be purified and the bad luck lifted from it," Bob pointed out.

"Sure," Pete agreed. "And you also said many collectors would be afraid to risk it even after fifty years."

"I'm beginning to understand," Gus said, his eyes gleaming with excitement, "why Uncle August acted as he did. He hid The Fiery Eye and planned to keep it for fifty years. Then, when it was harmless, he would sell it. Finding himself dying just as the fifty years were up, he left it to me. I'm sure it's safe now."

"It may be safe," Jupiter said, "but Black Moustache has it. And at the moment I don't know how we're going to get it back from Black Moustache."

"The Ghost-to-Ghost Hookup!" Bob exclaimed. "We'll get thousands of kids looking for Black Moustache. When we find him, we'll—we'll—" He faltered, realizing he didn't have any idea what they would do then.

"Exactly," Jupiter nodded. "We couldn't just take it away from him. Anyway, do you realize how many men in this city answer to the description of Black Moustache? Hundreds at least. And that's not counting the fact that I suspect the black moustache is artificial, worn for a disguise."

"Then it's hopeless." Gus broke a long silence that followed Jupiter's remark.

Another silence followed. Even Jupiter did not seem to have any ideas. Then they heard a sharp ringing sound.

"The bell!" Bob exclaimed. "Some customer, Jupe."

"I'll go see what he wants." Jupiter rose and started toward the office. The others followed.

As they got out into the open, they could see the

customer standing beside his sleek black car, leaning on a cane and looking around.

"Oh-oh!" Pete whispered. "It's Three-Dots again!"

"I don't like this much," Bob whispered back.

But Jupiter was advancing toward the man and reluctantly they followed. Jupe, they noticed, had let his shoulders slump and was wearing his stupid look for the benefit of Three-Dots.

"Good evening, boys," Three-Dots said. He smiled. It was not a nice smile. "I have just been examining —that!"

With his cane he pointed to the broken pieces of Augustus of Poland.

"It seems to be the remains of the bust of Augustus, in which I was especially interested. I believe I requested you to telephone me if it was returned."

"Yes, sir," Jupiter said. "Only it got broken."

"And I wonder how it got broken?" Three-Dots' smile was like the smile of a tiger about to eat a nice, plump boy. "I have noticed with special interest the small cavity inside the broken chunks. Something was hidden in that bust."

"Yes, sir," Jupiter said, his voice dull. "A customer dropped it and it broke. He picked up something. We didn't get a good look at it."

Which was perfectly true. They hadn't. Though they had been pretty sure what Black Moustache had picked up.

"This customer," Three-Dots said. "Would he have been a man with large glasses and a black moustache?"

Jupiter nodded. Pete and Bob and Gus exchanged startled glances.

"And—" the tall man continued—"would the object the gentleman picked up from the bust have looked like this?"

With an abrupt movement he took something from his pocket and tossed it down on the table beside the broken bust. It was small and eye-shaped and shone with a red glow.

The Fiery Eye!

Even Jupiter gulped slightly as he answered.

"Yes, sir, it looked like that."

"Hmmm." The man leaned on his cane and looked at them all. "You have all heard of The Fiery Eye, I imagine. You have all heard of the dire fate that follows any who possess it."

There didn't seem to be any good answer to that, so they remained silent. They were wondering, though, how Three-Dots could have The Fiery Eye now, when Black Moustache had made off with it less than an hour before.

"I wish to show you something."

Three-Dots lifted his cane. He twisted the handle. The sword blade thrust out from the end of the cane. He looked at it with disapproval.

"Careless," he remarked. "I did not clean it properly."

From his pocket he took a tissue and wiped the sword blade. Something red and sticky came off on the tissue.

"Blood is very bad for fine steel," he said, while chills ran up and down the boys' spines. "However—"

He reached forward and put the edge of his razor-sharp sword blade against The Fiery Eye. He drew the blade sharply across the ruby. Then he held the stone out to Jupiter.

"Examine it," he said. "Tell me what you see."

Jupiter held it up so he could see it better. The others crowded around him. For a moment they couldn't see anything special. Then Bob spotted it, just as Jupiter did. The sword blade had made a fine scratch across the stone.

"The ruby is scratched," Jupiter said. "I don't understand. Rubies are harder than steel. The steel shouldn't be able to scratch it."

"Ah!" Three-Dots seemed pleased. "So you are not as stupid as you have been pretending. I did not think you were. In fact, I was quite sure you were a very astute young man." As Jupiter bit his lip in chagrin at giving himself away, he added, "Now—deduce for me the meaning of that scratch."

Jupiter was silent, studying the red stone. "It's

scratched because it isn't a real ruby," he said at last. "It's an imitation, made out of paste."

"Exactly!" Three-Dots' voice was sharp. "It's a paste imitation that I took from the gentleman with the black moustache. The real Fiery Eye is still to be found. As it is hidden inside a bust of Augustus, there must be another Augustus in the group which has been sold. I am depending on you to find it for me."

He paused and fixed them each in turn with his eyes.

"I order you all to find me that other Augustus!" he said. "Or else—but I prefer not to make threats. I think you understand me. Phone me as soon as you locate it."

With that he stepped into the waiting car and in a moment was gone, leaving them all staring at one another.

"He—he must have killed Black Moustache to get the ruby from him," Pete said. "Boy, how did he know so quickly that Black Moustache had it?"

"The mystery gets deeper," Jupiter said. "Why did Mr. August put a fake ruby inside the bust of Augustus of Poland? Was he fooled all along, and thought it was the real ruby? Or did he do it on purpose to mislead a searcher? If so, did he put the real ruby into another bust? Because we know there isn't another one of Augustus and—"

"That's just it!" Bob burst out. "There is!"

They looked at him. Jupiter blinked.

"I just remembered," Bob said. "Dad told me earlier. It's Octavian! He was a Roman emperor and his other name was Augustus. When Gus's great-uncle wrote, 'In August is your fortune,' he had to mean the bust of Octavian, because the month of August is actually named after him! It's Octavian we have to find!"

IMPORTANT CALL
FROM A GHOST _____ 9

"I SAY we forget all about The Fiery Eye!" Pete said emphatically. "It's supposed to have killed at least fifteen men, and I don't want the score to become fifteen men and four boys."

"Pete's right," Gus said. "I'm not sure I'd want The Fiery Eye even if we could find it. It does seem rather a risky thing to own."

"Look at what happened to Black Moustache!" Pete exclaimed. "He had it for less than an hour and —zick! They got him!"

Bob didn't say anything. He was watching Jupe, and Jupe's face had a stubborn look.

"We haven't found The Fiery Eye yet," Jupe said. "So I don't think we are in any danger. Anyway, not yet."

"Let's put it to a vote," Pete suggested. "I vote we abandon the case now. All in favor say aye!"

"Aye! Aye! Aye!" The word rang out several times. However, it was spoken by Blackbeard, the trained mynah bird whose cage hung over the desk in Head-quarters.

Nobody but Blackbeard voted with Pete. Gus was silent because he was an outsider and Bob was silent because he had faith in Jupiter. Besides, Jupe was awfully hard to outvote and Bob already knew Jupe wanted to keep on with the case.

"Dead men tell no tales!" Blackbeard called out and laughed shrilly.

"Quiet, you!" Pete snapped. "Do you have to rub it in?" He turned to Jupiter. "All right," he said. "What do we do now? Shouldn't we phone the police to report what happened to Black Moustache?"

"We have no proof," Jupiter said. "Without evidence they wouldn't believe us. Naturally, we'll tell all we know if Black Moustache is found, though.

"As things now stand, we only have one line of action open to us. We have to try to locate the bust of Octavian, and the only way to do that is to use the Ghost-to-Ghost Hookup. As it is now after seven, most of our friends should be home. I propose we start phoning and get the hookup under way."

With that decided, they wasted no more time talking. Jupiter called five of his friends, asking them to phone back after ten o'clock the next morning if they knew of Octavian's whereabouts. Then Bob phoned five of his friends and Pete phoned five of his. When they had finished, they knew all of the fifteen were phoning five more friends, who in turn would phone five more, and so on until hundreds or even thousands of boys and girls in Rocky Beach, Hollywood and Los Angeles had been reached.

As The Three Investigators had used the Ghost-to-Ghost Hookup successfully before, most of those contacted were familiar with the procedure and enjoyed helping in a mystery investigation, even though they didn't know Jupiter, Pete or Bob personally.

When they had finished telephoning, Jupiter invited Gus to spend the night with him rather than go back to his hotel room in Hollywood, and Gus accepted. Pete and Bob got their bikes and started homeward, riding together the first part of the way.

"Do you think we'll find this Octavian statue?" Pete asked as they rode.

"If we don't, somebody is going to be awfully surprised some day," Bob answered. "I mean, if they put the bust out in the garden and the weather dissolves the plaster, some morning they will come out to find a priceless ruby lying on their lawn."

"Or if they keep it inside the house, someday it will probably get thrown out and the ruby will go to the junk heap," Pete observed.

They separated, and Bob rode on home. He found his father looking with annoyance at the telephone.

"I've been trying to call the newspaper," his father said as Bob came in. "And for some reason all the circuits out of Rocky Beach have been constantly busy for the last half-hour. That doesn't sound possible, but it's true."

Bob knew the reason, but he thought it better not to mention that the Ghost-to-Ghost Hookup was in operation. Whenever the hookup was being used, the local telephone business got a big and unexpected boost.

He went on up to bed, but it was quite a while before he could fall asleep. When he did, he had vivid dreams of Indian tribesmen on horseback, all carrying sword-canes.

When he opened his eyes, the sun was well up and he smelled bacon frying downstairs. He scrambled into his clothes, and went downstairs two steps at a time. He found his mother in the kitchen.

"Hi, Mom!" he said. "Any messages from Jupiter?"

"Now, let me think . . ." His mother put her finger to her chin and pretended to be in deep thought. "There was one. Could it have been, 'The cow jumped over the moon and the dish ran away with the spoon'?"

Bob frowned. That wasn't part of the message code Jupiter had worked out. Then he saw his mother smiling and realized she was joking with him.

"Aw, Mom!" he said. "What was it really?"

"Now that I think harder," his mother told him, "it was 'Rustle and bustle, this is the score. Somebody's needed to mind the store.' Now honestly, Robert, couldn't you boys communicate in ordinary language?" Then she added, "No, I suppose it's more fun this way. I won't ask what it means, but something tells me you are all working on another one of your cases."

"Yes, Mom," Bob said absentmindedly as he sat down at the dinette table. "Rustle and bustle" meant to get to the salvage yard as fast as he could, but not on top emergency. "Somebody's needed to mind the store" meant that Jupiter needed him to stay in Headquarters by the telephone because Jupe had gone off someplace. Where, Bob wondered, had Jupe gone this morning?

"Well, is that all you're going to say?" his mother asked, putting a plate of bacon and eggs and toast in front of him. "Just 'yes, Mom'?"

"Oh, excuse me," Bob said, his thoughts interrupted. "I mean, yes, we're on a case. We're looking for a bust of a Roman emperor named Octavian that got sold by mistake. It belongs to an English boy named Gus and we're trying to locate it."

"That's nice," his mother said. "Now eat all of your eggs, a bust isn't going to run away. That's one thing about statues, they stay put."

Bob couldn't tell her that that was the trouble with this bust—it was very elusive. However, he ate his breakfast, then rode as swiftly as he could to the salvage yard. There he found Mrs. Jones in the office and Hans and Konrad busy straightening up around the yard.

"Good morning, Bob," Mathilda Jones greeted him. "Jupiter and Pete and that English boy rode off on bicycles half an hour ago. Jupiter left a message for you back there where his machinery is."

Bob hastened back to the workshop section. There was a note propped up on the printing press: *Bob: Man the bells. We are on a scouting expedition. First Investigator J. Jones.*

"Man the bells" meant to stay by the telephone for any calls from their "ghosts." But where could Jupe and the others have gone on a scouting expedition, Bob wondered as he crawled through Tunnel Two and let himself into the little office of Headquarters.

He could hear the telephone ringing as he pushed up the trap door. His watch said five minutes to ten. Some "ghost" was early in reporting. Bob scrambled the last few feet and grabbed up the phone.

"Three Investigators, Bob Andrews speaking," he panted.

"Hello," answered a boy's voice. "This is Tommy Farrell and maybe I have some information for you. My married sister bought a little statue at The Jones Salvage Yard and she has it out in her garden now."

"What's the name of it?" Bob asked eagerly. "Is it Octavian?"

"Gee, I don't remember. Hang on for a minute while I go look."

Bob waited, his heart pounding. Had the Ghost-to-Ghost Hookup been successful so soon? If Tommy Farrell's sister had Octavian—

Then the boy's voice spoke again.

"Not Octavian," he said. "The name is Bismarck. That help any?"

"Thanks a lot, Tommy," Bob said, disappointed. "But we really need Octavian. We appreciate your calling, though."

"Okay." The other boy hung up and Bob put the phone back in its cradle. Then, not having anything else to do until it rang again, he sat down at the typewriter and typed up all his notes on the case so far. When he had finished, he looked at his wristwatch and saw that it was almost noon. There hadn't been any more calls. This time the Ghost-to-Ghost Hookup was a failure.

"Bob! Bob Andrews!" Mathilda Jones' powerful voice came in through the open skylight. "Jupiter isn't back but lunch is ready. You might as well eat."

"I'll be right there," Bob called into the microphone.

He started for Tunnel Two and had the trap door open when the telephone began to ring. He scrambled back, grabbed up the phone and breathlessly said, "Hello! Three Investigators. Bob Andrews."

"You wanted to know about a bust of Octavian," a girl's voice answered. "Well, my mother has it, but she tried putting it in the garden and she thinks it looks silly. She said she's going to give it away to a neighbor."

"Please don't let her do that!" Bob cried. "Our motto is that every customer must be satisfied. We'll come out to your house just as soon as we can and refund her money. I'll also bring another bust in case she thinks it would look better."

He took down the name and the address, which was in Hollywood, a good many miles away, and hung up. Then he looked anxiously at his watch.

If only Jupe would hurry back. They had located Octavian—but if they didn't act fast they'd lose him again!

P E T E led the way as, puffing slightly, the three boys pushed their bikes up a small rise and out into the open part of Dial Canyon.

The canyon was narrow and quite high up in the hills northwest of Hollywood. Only one road led to it, an unpaved one that ended in this flat section. Here, the late Horatio August's house sat in a large area of long, untended grass.

It had been Jupiter's idea to visit the house. He didn't know exactly what they were looking for, but he thought they should see the house where Gus's great-uncle had lived.

It had taken them longer than they expected to ride through the hills. Now it was nearly noon, and the sun was high and hot overhead. They paused to wipe the sweat off their faces and to look at the empty home of Horatio August.

Three stories tall, of timber and plaster, it was very impressive standing all by itself in the open. Nothing moved and there was no sign of life. They rode up to the front door and left their bicycles on the grass.

"We haven't got the key, but there ought to be some way to get in," Pete said. "After all, we have permission from Mr. Dwiggins."

"We could break a window to obtain entrance," Gus suggested.

"We don't want to do any damage if we can help it," Jupiter answered, "even though the house is soon going to be torn down. I have a bunch of keys with me—" He hauled from his pocket a fat bunch of keys which had accumulated at the salvage yard over a period of years. "Let's see if one of these will open the door, before we try anything else."

They walked up three steps to the front door and Pete tried the knob. To his surprise the door swung open silently.

"It's open already!" he said. "It wasn't even latched."

"That's odd," Jupiter said, frowning.

"Perhaps Mr. Dwiggins left it open after he was here the other day," Pete suggested. "Or maybe someone else did. It doesn't matter—people don't worry much about locking up empty houses."

They walked into a dark hallway. On either side were two big rooms, dusty and empty, except for some scraps of paper on the floor.

Jupiter entered the one which he deduced had been the living room. He looked around, but there didn't seem to be anything much to see. There was no furniture. The room was paneled in dark walnut, which still shone despite a layer of dust.

There was nothing to see, so he turned and strolled across the hall into the opposite room. This one had apparently been a library, because built-in bookshelves towered around three sides of the room. Now they were empty of everything but dust. Jupiter stood in the middle of the room, looking at the shelves. "Ah!" he said, after a long look.

"What do you mean, ah?" Pete asked. "I can't see anything to ah at."

"You must train your powers of observation if you're ever going to be a first-rate investigator," Jupe said. "Observe that section of bookcase directly in front of me."

Pete stared at it. "I don't see anything but dust," he said at last.

"At the end," Jupiter told him, "it extends outward beyond the next section by a quarter of an inch. I consider that very significant."

He walked over and tugged at the section of bookcase. Slowly it swung open. Behind it was the black opening of a narrow door.

"A secret room behind the bookcases!" Jupe said.

"The bookcase door was not quite shut."

"Wow!" Pete exclaimed. "We've found something."

"We should have brought flashlights," Jupiter said. "That was careless of me. Pete, go out and get the electric headlight off your bicycle."

In a moment Pete was back and handed Jupe the bicycle headlamp.

"I guess you'll want to go first," he said.

"There can't be anything alarming in there," Jupiter said. "Not in a house empty this long."

Pete wasn't so sure. They had encountered a couple of secret rooms before in their investigations, and one of them had held a skeleton. But Jupe turned on the bright beam and marched into the tiny room behind the bookcase, and Pete and Gus followed.

They took no more than three steps and stopped.

There was no skeleton in this room, nor anything else. It was completely empty. Shelves on the wall suggested that books had once been kept in this room, but they were gone.

"Nothing," Pete said in disappointment.

"Nothing?" Jupe asked and Pete looked around again.

"I don't see anything," he said.

"Because you're looking for the wrong thing," Jupe said. "What you're looking at is so commonplace, so ordinary, that your mind doesn't realize how extraordinary it really is."

Pete blinked again. He still didn't see anything.

"All right, tell me," he said. "What's so unusual I can't see it?"

"He means there's a door," Gus said. Pete saw it now—an ordinary doorknob, and the crack around a door set into the wall. It wasn't meant to be hidden. He just hadn't noticed the doorknob because every room has a door, and seeing one in here hadn't registered on him.

Jupiter was already turning the knob. The narrow door opened easily and by the beam of the light they could see wooden steps slanting downward.

"It looks as if the steps go down to the cellar," Jupiter said. "We might as well try them and see where we come out."

"Leave all the doors open then," Pete urged. "I don't want any closed doors in back of me."

Jupiter marched down the stairs, the others behind him. The walls on either side were so close they brushed their shoulders against the wood.

At the bottom Jupiter stopped. Another narrow door barred their way. It opened easily toward them. They stepped through into a small, stone-walled room where the air was cool and damp.

"We're in a cellar," Jupiter said, flashing the light around. They saw many curious slanting shelves which meant nothing to either Pete or Jupiter. However, Gus recognized their function.

"This is a wine cellar," he said. "Those shelves are for laying out the bottles of wine. Look, there's a broken bottle in one. This was Great-Uncle Horatio's private wine cellar."

Jupiter suddenly froze. He switched off the light and darkness enveloped them.

"What is it, Jupe?" Pete dropped his voice to a whisper.

"Sssh! Someone's coming. Look!"

Beyond the open door which led into the rest of the basement appeared a beam of light. Low voices could be heard.

"Let's get out of here!" Pete whispered and yanked at the knob of the door behind them.

He was too anxious. At his sudden yank, the knob came away in his hand. The voices and light came closer, and Pete's frantically clutching fingers found nothing to grasp.

They were trapped in the wine cellar!

"WE KNOW YOU'RE THERE!" _____ 11

THE VOICES came closer. Footsteps stopped just outside the wine cellar door. A flashlight made a gleam of light in the darkness beyond the door.

"We've already searched the wine cellar," said a deep voice. "No use going in there."

"We've searched the whole house," another, rougher voice said disgustedly. "We've spent a half hour on this cellar alone. Jackson, if you're holding out on us—"

"I'm not, I swear I'm not!" said a high-pitched, old man's voice. "If it's in this house we'd have found it. I tell you there aren't any hiding places I didn't know about. After all, I was Mr. Weston's—I mean Mr. August's butler for twenty years."

Jackson! Pete felt Jupiter stiffen. Mr. Dwiggins had said a couple named Jackson had been Gus's great-uncle's only servants.

"You'd better be sure, Jackson," said the first voice. "We aren't playing a game for marbles. This is big money and you'll get your share when we find the Eye."

"I've told you everything I know, really I have!" Mr. Jackson said pleadingly. "He must have hidden it someplace when Agnes and I were out of the house. I'm not sure he trusted us at the end—although we served him faithfully all those years. He began to act a little odd, as if he felt he was being spied on."

"He was smart, he didn't trust anybody. Not with a stone like the Eye to hide," the second, rough voice said. "I wish I could figure what he meant by planting that phony stone inside the head of Augustus, though."

The boys were listening with eager interest, almost forgetting their perilous position. If the speakers knew about the fake Fiery Eye, that must mean they were accomplices of either Black Moustache or Three-Dots. The next words cleared up this question for them.

"Poor Hugo! When that guy with those three dots finished with him, Hugo didn't feel so hot," the rough voice said, and chuckled.

At the tone and the laugh Pete felt chills go down his spine. He remembered that gleaming sword blade and the red stain that had come off it.

"Never mind Hugo," said the deep voice. "Why was a fake ruby inside the head of Augustus? Only to throw a false trail, I bet. I think the ruby is hidden right here in this house."

"If it is, gentlemen, you'll have to tear the whole house down to find it," Mr. Jackson said. "I swear to you I have no more ideas of where to look. Please let me go back to my wife in San Francisco. I've done all I could, really I have."

"We'll think about it," said the rough voice. "Maybe we'll let you go. The person I wish I had my hands on is that fat smarty at the junkyard! I've asked around about him and they say that kid has brains like a computer, even if he does look stupid. I'll bet a red nickel he knows a lot more than he's telling."

"Well, there's no way we can get at him," Deep Voice said. "Or maybe there is. Come on, let's go upstairs and figure our next move."

"What about the secret staircase and the little room?" asked Rough Voice. "We ought to search those again. They must mean something."

"Too obvious," Deep Voice said. "Like Jackson told us, it used to be just an ordinary stairway down to the wine cellar from the library. Right, Jackson?"

"Yes, indeed," Mr. Jackson said. "Twenty years ago Mr. August put in the bookshelves and just for fun he made them into a secret door for the stairway. But he only used it to go to his wine cellar at night. He always said that as a boy in England he dreamed of living in a big house with a secret staircase."

"There you are," said Deep Voice. "Let's get back upstairs. This dark cellar makes me feel gloomy."

The light moved away. In a moment the three boys heard footsteps going up wooden stairs. Then a door slammed shut. They were alone again in the cellar.

"Whew!" Pete said. "I thought they had us. They sounded like tough customers."

"My word!" Gus exclaimed. "Did you hear how that one just laughed when he talked about what Three-Dots did to his companion?"

"What do you say, Jupe—who were they?" Pete asked. "Jupe—are you in a trance or something?"

Jupe came to himself with a little jump.

"I was thinking," he said. "The two men must have learned about The Fiery Eye from Mr. Jackson, and are making Mr. Jackson help them try to get it before Three-Dots does."

Pete nodded. "But how are we getting out of here? We're trapped."

"I think it will be safest to wait until they leave. Let's find the cellar door, though, and be ready to make a break for freedom at the first possible moment."

With Jupe leading the way, they emerged into a big square cellar with low beams overhead. There were no windows. Down at one end was a big oil tank for the oil-burning furnace next to it. Other than that, there wasn't much to see.

There was, however, a flight of wooden steps leading up to a door, and they tiptoed up them. Jupe

cautiously tried the doorknob. The knob turned, but
the door refused to open. Jupe rattled it slightly, then
drew back.

"It's bolted on the other side," he said. "We're
locked in."

For a moment they were all silent. If they were
locked in the cellar, and the men above went away
and left them there, who knew when someone else
would come? It might be days—maybe not until the
workmen came to tear the house down.

Jupiter broke the silence.

"There's the door to the secret staircase," he said.

"But the knob fell off on the other side," Gus objected. "I heard it fall. That door won't open, will it,
Pete?"

"Not for me it won't."

"Perhaps it will open for me," Jupe said.

They followed Jupe back into the wine cellar. Pete
held the light trained on the spot where the missing
doorknob should have been. Jupe got out his Swiss
knife, his pride and joy. He opened one blade, which
was a small screwdriver.

"When a knob is missing from an ordinary door,
a screwdriver will often turn the latch," Jupe remarked. He pushed the end of the screwdriver into
the hole where the shaft of the doorknob should have
gone. The edges of the blade caught the four-sided
piece of metal inside. Jupiter turned, the tongue of

the lock moved, and the door swung open.

"It's a very simple trick, but it's handy to know in emergencies," Jupe said as he emerged into the tiny space at the bottom of the secret stairway.

He had no sooner stepped outside the door than a flashlight beam blazed down the stairs. It illuminated Jupiter so brilliantly that he blinked his eyes, unable to see a thing.

"All right," Deep Voice boomed down at them. "We knew you kids were there. We saw your bicycles just now. So come on up, and come quietly, if you know what's good for you!"

JUPITER GETS
THE THIRD DEGREE ___ 12

JUPITER did not obey the shouted command.
He bent over and felt for the doorknob and shaft that
had fallen on this side of the door. As he turned,
fumbling on the floor, he bumped the open door and
closed it firmly.

Already two men were plunging down the steps
toward him.

"Grab him, Charlie!" called Deep Voice. "That's
Fatty! We want to talk to him."

Jupiter did not have time to resent being called
Fatty. Strong hands pinned his arms to his sides. A
moment later he was being hauled up the stairs by
his shirt front.

In the wine cellar, Pete and Gus heard the bumps
and thumps and exclamations as the two men pulled
Jupe up the stairs. They stared at each other in dismay.

"They've got First!" Pete said hollowly.

"He's putting up a jolly good struggle," Gus remarked as they heard one of the men grunt with pain.

At that exact moment, the sounds of struggle ceased. They heard Jupe's voice, muffled by the closed door. "All right, gentlemen, I'll go quietly. I am outnumbered and struggle will only prolong the inevitable sequence of events."

"Huh?" they heard Rough Voice answer. "What'd you say?"

"He said he's giving up because he knows he can't win," Deep Voice answered. "All right, Fatty, up those stairs. Make a false move and I'll clobber you."

"What about the other two?" asked Rough Voice.

"Leave them locked up," said Deep Voice. "This kid's the one we want to talk to."

Pete and Gus heard the bolt outside the wine cellar door slam into place, locking them in. Then footsteps went up the stairs and crossed the room above.

"He gave up," Gus sighed.

"Because he knew he couldn't lick them both," Pete defended Jupiter.

"Meanwhile he's a prisoner upstairs and we're prisoners down here," Gus said. "Both doors are bolted. We can't get out."

"Jupe will get us out some way," Pete assured him.

Jupiter, however, was not in a position to help himself, much less anyone else. Twisting his arm behind his back, Deep Voice marched him out into the kitchen, which held the only piece of furniture left in the house, a rickety old wooden chair not even worth buying for junk.

Deep Voice was short and rather fat. Rough Voice was big and burly. Both wore large horn-rimmed glasses and black moustaches, disguises similar to that of the first Black Moustache. All were obviously members of the same gang.

Deep Voice steered Jupe to the chair and forced him to sit down.

"There's some clothesline hanging up back of the house," he told his companion. "Get it."

The other man went out the kitchen door. Deep Voice expertly searched Jupiter and found his prized knife.

"Very pretty," he said. "Just right for slicing off an ear or two if we have to."

Jupiter was silent. Deep Voice sounded fairly well educated, not like a crook. Rough Voice sounded more like a thug, but it was plain that Deep Voice was in command.

In the doorway a small, nervous-looking man with gray hair and gold-rimmed spectacles appeared. This could only be Mr. Jackson.

"Now you mustn't hurt him," he said anxiously. "You promised me there would be no violence and no danger."

"Leave us alone!" Jupe's captor ordered curtly.

"There won't be any violence—provided, of course, Fatty here cooperates. Now beat it!"

The elderly man went back into the front room. Rough Voice came in with some lengths of clothes-line, and the two men proceeded to tie The First Investigator to the chair. They bound his arms to the arms of the chair, his legs to the front chair legs, and his waist to the back of the chair. When they had finished, he could hardly move.

"Now, boy," Deep Voice said, "we can talk. Where is the ruby?"

"I don't know," Jupiter replied. "We're looking for it, too."

"He's not cooperating," the other man said. He picked up Jupe's knife, which had been put down on a window sill. He opened the blade, which gleamed brightly. "Let me tickle him with this, Joe. Help him get in the mood for giving us the right answers."

"I'm handling this," his companion told him. "He probably doesn't know. But I bet he has some ideas. All right, Fatty, answer me this. Why was that stone in the bust of Augustus a fake?"

"I'm not sure," Jupiter said. Jupe had decided he might as well answer. He didn't know where The Fiery Eye was—at least he didn't know where the bust of Octavian that held it was—and if he could convince the two men he didn't know, they might release him.

"I think Mr. August put the false ruby into Augustus to mislead anyone who came looking for it," he added. "He wanted them to think they had found it, so he made it easy."

"Then where did he put the real ruby?" demanded Deep Voice, the one called Joe.

"In another of the busts," Jupe said. "One people wouldn't suspect so quickly. The bust of Octavian."

"Octavian, huh?" Rough Voice, called Charlie, asked. "And just why Octavian?"

"Of course!" Joe exclaimed. "Octavian was a Roman emperor the people called Augustus. Augustus—August—get it?"

"Well, yeah." Charlie scratched his head. "It begins to sound reasonable. Okay, kid, answer this. Where is Octavian?"

"I don't know," Jupiter answered. "My aunt sold it to someone, and she didn't keep any records of names and addresses. Anyone in Los Angeles or anywhere near here could have it."

Joe stared at him. Absentmindedly he rubbed his false moustache.

"That sounds as if it might be the truth," he said. "But I have another question for you. If you think the ruby is inside old Octavian, why aren't you out looking for him? Why did you come to this house?"

That was harder to answer. The truth was, Jupe had just had a hunch that he should inspect the house where the dead man had lived. He had no idea what kind of clue he was looking for.

"Since I didn't know where to look for Octavian," Jupiter said, "I decided to do the next best thing and look over this house. I might be wrong. Mr. August may not have hidden the ruby in Octavian at all."

"No, I think he did," Joe muttered. "It adds up that way. The message was a false trail to the first Augustus. Anyone who knew enough about history would go for Octavian instead. That's how the old man figured his great-nephew would think. So we have to find Octavian before anyone else does."

"And how are we going to do that?" Charlie demanded. "Anybody in or near Los Angeles could have it. We could spend a lifetime looking."

"That's a problem," his companion agreed. He fixed his gaze on Jupiter. "But that's not our problem. That's Fatty's problem. If he wants to get loose from that chair, it's up to him to figure out how we can find Octavian. Well, kid, what do you say?"

Jupiter was silent. He could tell them about the Ghost-to-Ghost Hookup. But that was a last resort.

"I haven't any idea where Octavian is," he said, trying to sound humble. "If I did, I'd have gone to try to get him back."

"Then you'd better start having some new ideas," Charlie said, his tone ugly. "You're supposed to be a whiz at thinking. So start the think works moving.

We can wait all day, if necessary. And maybe all night, too. If you want to get out of that chair and get your pals out of the cellar, come up with a good answer!"

At the moment Jupe didn't have any answer, good or otherwise. He thought swiftly. Bob ought to guess where they were. If they didn't show up, Bob would eventually come to this house with Hans, and maybe with Mr. Jones and Konrad. Sooner or later Bob should rescue them. But it might be a long time because Bob had instructions to stay by the telephone.

Jupiter decided to wait. Maybe Bob—

At that moment, little Mr. Jackson appeared in the kitchen doorway.

"Excuse me," he said nervously, "but the radio— I think your friends are trying to contact you. I heard a voice calling for Joe—"

Joe spun around. "The walkie-talkie!" he exclaimed. "Charlie, get it. That must be Hugo. Maybe there's action at the other end."

Charlie ran out of the room. Jupiter scarcely had time to wonder how Hugo could be calling anyone if Three-Dots had used the sword-blade on him when Charlie was back.

He was carrying a large portable walkie-talkie, much more powerful than the smaller instruments Jupe had made for himself and Bob and Pete. This was the kind of walkie-talkie that required a license to use, though obviously Charlie and Joe weren't worrying about that.

"It's Hugo, all right," Charlie said. He pressed a button on the walkie-talkie.

"Hugo," he said, "Charlie here. Do you read me? Come in. Come in."

He released the button and the walkie-talkie hummed. Then a voice spoke, raspy because of the distance.

"Charlie! Where have you been? I've been trying to raise you for ten minutes."

"We've been busy. What do you have to report?"

"Action at this end. The blond kid, the smaller one, just left the salvage yard in one of the trucks, with a yard helper driving. They're heading for Hollywood. We're following them."

Jupiter's heart leaped. Bob had decided to come look for them. In a little while he and Konrad or Hans would get there and then—

But his hopes were dashed by the next question and answer.

"Are they coming this way?"

"No, they're heading into town. They don't know we're following them."

"See where they go," Charlie instructed. "This may be a break." He looked across at Joe. "Anything you want to tell Hugo?" he asked.

"Yes! I bet the kid is going after Octavian. He's got a lead on the statue somehow. Tell Hugo to see if they pick up one of the plaster busts. If they do, he's to get it away from them any way he can!"

Charlie repeated the message into the walkie-talkie and signed off.

"There," he said. "That does it. Pretty smart of you, Joe, buying these walkie-talkies. I think they've just paid off—big. Now, kid—" he shoved his grinning face up close to Jupiter's—"we'll all just wait and see what happens."

BOB TAKES
THE TRAIL _____ 13

B O B had waited as long as he dared for Jupe and
Pete to come back. The "ghost" had said to hurry if
he wanted to get the bust of Octavian, and here it
was late afternoon and no sign of First and Second.
Maybe they were following up some new line of investigation, but he couldn't wait any longer, he finally
decided. He would have to handle this himself.

He got permission from Mrs. Jones to use the
smaller truck, with Hans to drive it. He also wangled
five dollars advance pay for future work he would do
around the yard. Finally, explaining that a customer
wasn't satisfied with one of the busts but might be
willing to exchange it for another, he was allowed to
take the bust of Francis Bacon along, too.

Hans lugged it over to the truck and laid it down
on a bed of canvas. Bob added a heavy cardboard
box and a lot of newspaper to pack around the precious bust when they got it. Then they started out.

It was a forty-five minute drive to the address in

the outskirts of Hollywood. Their route took them on well-traveled roads through attractive residential sections. There was so much traffic that neither Bob nor Hans noticed that following them was a dark blue sedan with two men in it, both wearing large horn-rimmed glasses and black moustaches.

Presently Hans slowed down and Bob began inspecting the numbers on the houses they passed.

"That's it!" he yelled after a moment. "Stop here, Hans."

"You bet," Hans rumbled.

He pulled the truck to a stop and Bob hopped out. Half a block behind them, the blue sedan stopped, the two occupants watching intently every move they made.

Hans climbed down beside Bob and picked up Francis Bacon. Carrying him under his arm, he followed Bob to the front door.

Bob's ring was answered by a girl with pretty, freckled features.

"You're one of The Three Investigators!" she exclaimed, and Bob was pleased at the slight touch of awe in her voice. "And you want my mother's bust of Octavian for some strange and probably secret reason, don't you? Come in. I had a simply terrible time keeping her from giving Octavian away and I finally had to tell her it was made of a deadly radioactive plaster and you were security agents coming to get it to keep it from doing any harm."

All this came out in such a fast burst of words that Bob had a little trouble following it. Hans just blinked. But the girl was already leading them around the house into an attractive tiled patio with a little fountain in the middle. Bob's heart gave a leap. In one corner stood the bust of Octavian, looking rather silly under a tall rose bush.

A slender woman was clipping the rose bush. She turned, but already the girl was talking.

"Mother, these are The Three Investigators I was telling you about. At least this is one of them and his helper. He's come to take back Octavian and relieve you of the anxiety of harboring a dangerous plaster bust."

"Don't mind Liz." The woman smiled. "She lives in a world all her own, full of mysterious spies and sinister criminals. I didn't believe a word she said about Octavian being radioactive, but he doesn't look well in the patio and I was going to give him away. I waited for you because Liz said it was very important for you to get him back."

"Thank you, ma'am," Bob said. "Octavian was sort of sold by mistake. If you'd like another bust instead, we've brought Francis Bacon along."

"No," the woman said. "At first I thought it would be a cute idea to have a bust in the patio, but I see it doesn't look as well as I expected."

"Then we'll refund your money," Bob said. He dug the five-dollar bill from his pocket and presented it.

"That's certainly very fair," the woman said. "Now you can take Octavian away. I think I'll get an Italian vase to decorate the patio instead."

"Can you carry both busts, Hans?" Bob asked.

"I got two hands, can carry two busts," Hans said. "Easy like pie." He scooped up the precious Octavian and held him under his left arm. "Now what, Bob?"

"We'll take him out and pack him in the box," Bob said. "Tie it up tight. Then—"

"Do you have to go right away?" Liz asked. "I mean, this is the first time I've ever met a real investigator, and there are just millions of things I want to ask you."

"Well—" Bob hesitated. It was rather fun hearing Liz talk. Besides, if she was so interested in mysteries and investigations . . . "You go on and pack Octavian, Hans," he said. "I'll be right there. Do a good job."

"Sure thing, Bob," Hans said. He tramped off with a bust under each arm, leaving Bob talking—or rather listening, for Liz was firing questions at him without waiting for answers.

Hans carefully laid the two busts in the back of the truck and began the thorough packing job Bob had ordered. Every move he made was watched by the two men in the car. The one named Hugo kept up a continuous report to his two accomplices across the hills at Horatio August's house.

"The big guy is packing the bust now," he said tensely into the walkie-talkie. "It has to be Octavian —the kid wouldn't come here for any other bust. He's still inside the patio. There—the box is all tied up, nice and neat, and the big guy is waiting for the kid to come out."

Tied to the kitchen chair, Jupiter could hear every word as the two men listened. The one named Joe barked back instructions.

"Get that box off the truck!" he said. "Listen, I have an idea. Stage an accident. Hugo, you walk in front of the truck when it starts up, and pretend it's hit you. Scream and yell. The man and the boy will hop down to see how badly you're hurt and—"

"Hold it, hold it!" interrupted the voice of the distant Hugo. "That won't be necessary. The big guy is going back into the patio. The truck is unguarded. Frank and I are on our way."

The walkie-talkie was silent. Inwardly, Jupiter groaned. Just as Bob had regained Octavian, they were going to lose the bust again!

Hans walked back into the patio. Bob and Liz were still talking, or at least Liz was talking and Bob was answering when she gave him a chance.

"Look, don't you ever need a girl operative?" Liz was asking eagerly. "I'm sure you must on some of your investigations. There are times when a girl would be a big help. You could call on me. I'm a terrific actress. I can use make-up to disguise myself, and I can change my voice and—"

"Excuse, Bob," Hans rumbled. "Just to remind you, Mrs. Mathilda said not to stay away with the truck too long."

"Oh, sure, Hans!" Bob exclaimed. "Sorry, Liz, I've got to go. Maybe we might need a girl operative sometime. If we do, I'll call you."

"Here's my telephone number." Liz was following him, scribbling on a card in her hand as she walked. "There. Liz Logan, that's the name. I'll be waiting to hear from you. Wow, I can hardly wait to take part in a real investigation!"

Bob took the card and climbed into the truck beside Hans, not even noticing the blue sedan that passed them. He was thinking that Liz seemed like a pretty nice sort, and maybe a girl could help them sometime. It was true Jupiter had little use for girls, but if the right occasion ever arose, he'd suggest they call Liz Logan.

She waved good-bye and he waved back, not even glancing into the back of the truck. He and Hans headed back for the salvage yard, unaware that they had lost Octavian almost as soon as they had recovered him.

Jupiter knew, though. The walkie-talkie began to crackle and then speak. He heard Hugo's voice.

"Got it!" Hugo was saying. "The big lug went inside the patio and Frank and I grabbed that box from the truck the second he was out of sight. I don't think they even know it's gone."

"Good work!" Joe snapped back. "Take it to the hideout and don't open it until we get there. Over and out."

"Roger. Over and out."

The walkie-talkie was silent. Joe gave Jupiter Jones a one-sided grin.

"Well, kid, I guess that does it," he said. "We've got the stone. So we don't have to question you any more. But just to be on the safe side, we're going to leave you three kids safe here until we've got the stone and covered our tracks. Don't worry, we'll phone your buddy to come get you—but later, maybe tonight."

He and his companion went out the kitchen door, taking Mr. Jackson with them. Mr. Jackson gave Jupiter a last long glance, as if to say he was sorry he couldn't help. Then all three got into a car that had been out of sight behind the house and drove away.

As soon as they were gone, Jupiter raised his voice.

"Pete! Gus! Can you hear me?"

"Is that you, Jupe?" Pete's muffled voice came from beneath him. "What's up? Can you let us out of here? The batteries in the light are going dead!"

"Sorry, Second," Jupe called back. "I'm in a fix myself. I'm wrapped up like a mummy. We're stuck here and the Black Moustache gang has Octavian."

A STARTLING
DISCOVERY ————————

J U P I T E R sat tied tightly to the chair and pondered. In stories, when someone was tied up there was
always a convenient way to get loose. You could find
an old knife and saw the ropes against the blade to
cut them. Or there was a piece of broken glass that
could be used the same way. There was always something.

But he had nothing. Oh, there was his knife, all
right. It was lying on the window sill. But he couldn't
reach it. If he could have reached it, he couldn't have
got it open. If he could have got it open, he couldn't
have sawed the ropes against the blade because his
arms were tied separately to the arms of the chair.

Jupiter sat and thought, trying to figure out some
way to get loose. He wasn't exactly afraid of starving
to death, because someone would come eventually,
but it might take a long time.

Underneath him he heard bumps and thumps.
Pete and Gus were flinging themselves against the

bolted door, trying to break loose. Presently he heard their voices.

"Hey, Jupe, Jupe! Can you hear me?"

"Very clearly, Second," Jupiter answered loudly. "What success?"

"None. This door is solid. All we've done is bruise our shoulders. Say, it's awful dark down here."

"Have patience, Second. I'm trying to think of some way to escape."

"Okay, First. But think fast! I think there are rats down here."

Jupiter bit his lip to help his thinking processes. He wriggled impatiently in his chair. It creaked and groaned as he shifted his weight around.

Outside the kitchen window he could see time passing. It was as if he watched a clock. The tall, thin peak on the west side of the canyon threw a shadow across the lawn, and he could almost see that shadow grow longer and longer as the sun moved down in the west.

He moved some more, testing his bonds. They were tight, but the chair creaked and groaned again.

Then an electric light bulb seemed to go off in Jupiter's brain. Once he had sat on a creaky old chair and it had collapsed under his weight. If he could make this chair collapse—

He began to fling his body back and forth as violently as he could. The back of the chair moved. The arms wobbled. But they refused to break apart. Deliberately he threw himself sideways. He fell over with a thump on the floor. A leg of the chair splintered—the one his right leg was tied to.

He kicked hard and the leg of the chair slid out of the ropes, leaving them loose around his own leg. He had one leg free! Now he used this leg to lift himself up and slam the back of the chair to the floor again. He rolled over and put his full weight on the loose arms of the chair. They groaned, and the left arm pulled loose from the back. He jerked again and the whole chair arm came free.

Now he could reach over to move the right arm back and forth. As he struggled with the chair, thumping and bumping on the floor, Pete's alarmed voice came up from the cellar.

"Jupe! What's wrong? Are you in a fight or something?"

"I am fighting an enraged chair," Jupe puffed back. "And I think I'm winning. Give me another couple of minutes."

He strained, pushed, kicked. Now the chair was almost apart. Back, seat, arms, legs—all separated from each other. Most of the chair parts were still tied to him, but they were loose. He could crawl to the window, get his knife now, get it open. He could move his right arm enough to saw the ropes that tied the pieces of chair to his other arm. In a minute more he was able to stand up and kick himself free from the ropes and the broken chair.

With a feeling of triumph he stretched his aching muscles.

"It's all right, Second!" he called out. "I'm coming now."

Stairs from the kitchen led down to the cellar. He unbolted the wooden door. Pete and Gus blinked up at him in the light that came down the stairs.

"Gosh!" Pete said fervently as they came up. "I'm glad to see you, Jupe. How'd you get loose?"

"It was merely a case of mind over matter," Jupiter said, somewhat loftily. "Now we'd better get away from here. I don't expect Joe and his friend to come back yet, but they might. In any case, we want to get back to the salvage yard. Bob recovered the bust of Octavian—"

"He did? Terrific!" Pete exclaimed.

"That's very good news!" Gus chimed in.

"But the Black Moustache gang got it away again," Jupiter finished. "I'll tell you all about it as we ride home."

They scrambled out of the house and found their bikes. In a moment they were pedaling back toward Rocky Beach. As they rode, Jupiter told them all that had happened while they were locked in the cellar, ending with how Bob had apparently recovered Octavian, and how the Black Moustaches had gotten it from him.

"Golly, to have it right in our hands and lose it again," Pete mourned. "That bust is jinxed!"

"I hope it isn't the bad luck that follows The Fiery Eye," Gus suggested soberly.

"If it is, it ought to hit the Black Moustaches, not us," Jupiter said. "What I'm wondering about is the one they called Hugo. He sounded healthy, yet if Three-Dots used that sword-blade on him, he shouldn't be. Healthy, I mean."

"It's a puzzle," Pete agreed. "But what bothers me is how we're ever going to get our hands on Octavian again. Gus, I'm afraid your inheritance is gone."

Glumly they rode along through increasing traffic. It took quite a long time to get back to The Jones Salvage Yard. The sun was setting and they had remembered they hadn't eaten lunch and were ravenously hungry by the time they rode through the yard's main gate.

No one was in sight except Bob, Hans and Konrad. The two big yard helpers were busy in a far corner stacking lumber. The small truck was parked beside the office, waiting to be put away. Bob was listlessly painting some iron garden furniture from which he had rubbed the rust.

"Bob looks really discouraged," Pete said as they approached. "He feels pretty bad about losing Octavian."

"We all feel badly," Jupiter told him. "Let's try to cheer things up a bit. Let me do the talking to Bob."

As they approached, Bob looked up and tried to smile.

"Hi," he said. "I've been wondering where you were."

"We've been out to Gus's great-uncle's house," Jupiter told him as they put their bikes into a rack. "But we didn't find The Fiery Eye. Any developments at this end?"

"Well—" Bob began and hesitated, hating to tell them what had happened.

"Don't tell me," Jupiter said. "Let me try to deduce. Look me in the eye, Bob. That's it. Don't blink. Let me try to see in your eyes what it is you don't want to talk about."

Pete and Gus watched with amusement as Jupiter stared solemnly into Bob's eyes, then put his fingers to his forehead as if thinking deeply.

"It's coming to me," he said. "I'm getting the picture. There was a phone call—yes, a phone call from one of our ghosts. Octavian had been located. You went to get him—you and Hans in the smaller truck. You went to—let me see—yes, you went to Hollywood. Am I correct so far?"

"That's what happened!" Bob exclaimed, his eyes popping. He had known Jupiter to make some amazing deductions in the past, but this beat anything he had ever done before. "Then——"

"No, don't interrupt," Jupe said. "I'm getting more pictures. You went into a house. Hans went with you. He carried a bust—to trade, I believe, if necessary. Then Hans came out again, carrying two busts. You had recovered the bust of Octavian. Hans carried Octavian to the truck and put him in a box and wrapped it up well. He went back to get you. You both emerged, got in the truck and drove off. When you got back here, you found that the box which held Octavian had mysteriously vanished, evaporated into thin air. Am I correct?"

"That's just how it happened!" Bob stared at him open-mouthed. "The box just disappeared. It couldn't have fallen off or anything—the tailgate of the truck was up. I don't know——"

At that moment Hans approached, carrying a bust under his arm. "This statue from the truck, Bob," he said, "what you want I do with it? Got to put the truck away for the night."

"Just put it on the bench," Bob replied. To Jupe he said, "It's Francis Bacon. I took it along to give the lady in case she wanted to trade for Octavian. But she took money instead."

Hans set the bust on the bench and walked away.

It was facing backwards and Pete, who knew Mrs. Jones liked things neat, walked over to turn it around.

"Jupe," Bob asked, "how did you know? About our getting Octavian back and—"

He was interrupted by Pete's shout. "Come here!" he said. "Come here and tell me if I'm seeing right."

They followed his pointing finger, and read the word inscribed in the base of the bust. *Octavian.*

"Octavian!" Gus exclaimed. "The Black Moustache gang didn't get him after all!"

"Hans packed the wrong bust!" Bob burst out. "That's what happened. He had two under his arms and when he got out to the truck, he put one down and packed the other—the wrong one. I didn't bother to look at this one because I was so depressed at losing Octavian—and I had him all along!"

Automatically they all looked behind them, as if Three-Dots or the Black Moustache gang might be coming in the gate at that moment. But all was quiet.

Even Jupiter was slightly flabbergasted by the new development, but he recovered quickly.

"Come on!" he said. "We'll take Octavian back to the workshop and open him up. Then we'll hide The Fiery Eye where no one can find it. We're taking no more chances!"

Pete, as the strongest of the four, carried the bust back to the workshop section and set it on the ground. Jupiter found a chisel and hammer.

"Look," he said, feeling the top of the bust. "Someone has bored a hole in here, put something in, and refilled it with plaster. The mark is faint, but clear. I'm sure we have The Fiery Eye at last."

"Less talk and more action!" Pete burst out. "Just give it a whack and let's see."

Jupiter set the edge of the chisel against the top of the bust and hit it with the hammer. On the second blow the bust split in two, and a small round wooden box which had been embedded inside fell to the ground. Pete pounced on it and handed it to Jupiter.

"Open it, Jupe!" he urged. "Let's see this ruby that's been hidden for fifty years . . . Well, what are you waiting for? Afraid of the bad luck curse?"

"No," the First Investigator said slowly. "But the box doesn't feel heavy enough. However—"

He twisted the top off the round box. They all peered in. There was no flaming red stone inside. Just a curled-up slip of paper. Very slowly Jupiter took it out and spread it open. On it were just seven words. They said:

Delve deeper. Time is of the essence.

SOLVING THE MESSAGE _____ 15

B O B had a hard time getting to sleep that night. The events of the day had been just too exciting and puzzling. And to end up finding only a piece of paper inside Octavian! It was just too much.

Jupiter had stared at the paper, obviously disappointed. He had been sure they had hold of The Fiery Eye at last, and Jupe hated to be wrong. Then he read it aloud: "Delve deeper. Time is of the essence."

"But that's what the original message said!" Pete burst out.

"Apparently we haven't dug—delve means dig— deep enough into the riddle," Jupiter said. "Mr. August used these busts just to fool anybody who learned about the message and started looking for the ruby. Gus, he expected you to understand somehow."

"But I don't," Gus answered, wrinkling his brow. "I'm totally baffled. Great-Uncle Horatio probably expected my father to be with me, helping me solve the message. But Father couldn't come. We didn't have enough money for two, and he had to tend to his business."

"Let's read it again," Jupiter suggested, and Gus got the paper from his pocket. Jupe spread it out and they all read it.

> *To August August, my great-nephew:*
>
> *August is your name and August is your fame and in August is your fortune. Let not the mountain of difficulty in your way stop you; the shadow of your birth marks both a beginning and an ending.*
>
> *Delve deeply; the meaning of my words is for you alone. I dare not speak more plainly lest others find what is meant for you. It is mine. I paid for it and I own it, yet I have not dared its malevolence.*
>
> *But fifty years have passed and in half a century it should have purified itself. Yet still it must not be seized or stolen; it must be bought, given or found.*
>
> *Therefore take care, though time is of the essence. This and all my love I leave you.*
>
> *Horatio August*

"It still means nothing to me," Pete announced, frowning.

"I confess I don't understand it any better than before," Gus agreed. "In August is my fortune, it says. But if that doesn't mean in one of the busts of Augustus, what does it mean? Of course this is August, and tomorrow is my birthday. I was born at half past two on August 6th, my father told me. But how can my fortune be in the month of August?"

Jupiter pinched his lip. For once his mental machinery refused to respond. He sighed.

"I guess we'll have to sleep on it," he said. "But let me look at those pieces of Octavian again."

Pete handed him the two pieces of the bust, and Jupiter examined intently the hole in the center of the head where the little wooden box had been.

"Yes," he said. "Apparently Mr. August dug a hole into the bust and filled it with fresh plaster later. My theory is that he dug the hole to get The Fiery Eye *out* of the bust and put it someplace safer. He must have felt the bust wasn't a safe enough hiding place."

The other boys were silent. They had nothing to add to what Jupiter said.

"Well," the First Investigator said finally, "I guess there's nothing we can do now except eat. I've just realized I'm starved. Perhaps tomorrow will bring some new ideas."

Bob left them and biked home. He sat down at the dining room table to jot down notes about the day's happenings before he forgot them. He was writing of Jupiter, Gus and Pete's trip to Mr. August's old house

138 THE MYSTERY OF THE FIERY EYE

when it occurred to him that the name Dial Canyon
was rather unusual. Of course, a name could be anything, but still—

"Dad, did you ever hear of a place called Dial Canyon, north of Hollywood?" he asked. "It seems like an
odd name."

His father lowered the book he was reading.

"Dial Canyon?" he repeated. "Hmmm, I seem to
remember it, but I'm not sure. Let me look it up."

He went to the bookshelf for a large volume with
maps of the whole area.

"Dial Canyon—Dial Canyon," he repeated, turning the pages. "Let's see—yes, here it is. 'An isolated
little canyon, hard to reach, north of Hollywood. Formerly known as Sundial Canyon because from a certain angle one of the peaks around it looks like the
gnomon of a sundial.' A gnomon, Bob, is the upright
part of the sundial that casts the shadow on the sundial itself. So that's how your Dial Canyon got its name.
Formerly Sundial Canyon, and shortened to plain
Dial Canyon by everyday usage."

"Thanks, Dad," Bob said.

He made a few more notes, then he began to wonder if he ought to tell Jupiter what he had just learned.
It didn't seem important, but you never knew what
Jupe would find important. He decided to telephone
the Jones home. When Jupiter answered, Bob told
him what he had learned. For a moment there was

silence at the other end. Then he heard Jupe gulp slightly.

"Bob," the First Investigator said with suppressed excitement, "That's it. That's the clue!"

"What's the clue?" Bob asked, trying to figure out what Jupe was getting at.

"The clue I needed. Listen, you have to work in the library tomorrow morning, don't you? Well, be here right after lunch. One o'clock, say. I'll have everything ready."

"Ready for what?" Bob asked, but Jupiter had hung up. Bob went back to his notes, frowning. If what he had said was a clue, it didn't mean anything to him.

He went to bed still puzzled, and all next morning at the library he went about his work absentmindedly, still trying to figure out what was in Jupe's mind.

He didn't find out, however, until he reached The Jones Salvage Yard after lunch. There he found Jupe, Gus and Pete waiting for him. The smaller truck was ready to go and both Hans and Konrad were in the front seat. In the back were a couple of spades and some old canvas that made a seat for the boys. Jupiter had his camera.

"But where are we going?" Bob asked as the old truck bounced and jounced away from the salvage yard.

"That's what I want to know, too," Pete echoed.

"You're being awfully mysterious, Jupe. I think you ought to let us in on your plans. After all, we're your partners."

"We're going to test the message Mr. Horatio August left for Gus," Jupiter announced, looking rather pleased with himself. "Hans and Konrad are going with us as a security measure. I don't think anyone will dare attack us with them to contend with."

"All right, all right," Pete groaned. "Never mind all the words. Tell us what's up."

"Well, Bob gave me the clue when he told me Gus's great-uncle lived in Dial Canyon, which was formerly Sundial Canyon," Jupiter explained. "I should have figured it out for myself. After all, I sat there tied to a chair in the kitchen and saw the shadow of the peak move across the lawn just like the shadow of a sundial.

"You see, Gus, your great-uncle thought that you'd catch on, knowing how interested he was in different ways of telling time. He had an idea you or your father would put that together with the name of the canyon and the message and understand what he meant, while someone who didn't know about his hobby wouldn't."

"I still don't understand," Gus declared.

"Wait a minute!" Bob cried excitedly. "Sundial Canyon—the shadow of the natural sundial on the lawn marks the place where the ruby is buried, and

Gus has to delve for it. Is that the answer?"

"Correct, Records," Jupiter said.

"But it's a big lawn," Pete interjected. "How do we know the right spot?"

"The message tells us," Jupe answered. "Let's go over it again. May I have it, Gus? Thanks."

He spread out the message and read parts of it as the truck jounced along.

" 'August is your name and August is your fame and in August is your fortune'—that's to get Gus's attention to the word August, while just seeming mysterious to an outsider. Then, 'Let not the mountain of difficulty in your way stop you; the shadow of your birth marks both a beginning and an ending.'

"That's a sentence that seems to say one thing, and says another. Gus's great-uncle figured he would know that the mountain he meant is the peak above Dial Canyon, and that the shadow of his birth meant the shadow of the mountain at the time of his birth—that is, on August sixth at half past two in the afternoon. Correct, Gus?"

"That's right. I'm beginning to see it now, Jupiter. August—mountain—shadow—time of my birth—it all rather hits you in the eye as soon as you know you're talking about a giant sundial."

"The rest of the message is pretty plain," Jupiter stated. " 'Delve deeply' is clear enough. Most of the rest is just talk to help confuse an outsider. The phrase 'time is of the essence,' though, means two things. One is to hurry and find the ruby. The other goes back to the sundial idea; the right time is very important."

"Two-thirty today. That gives us hardly an hour!" Pete exclaimed.

"We'll make it. It's only a few more miles."

Pete stared hard behind them. They were alone on the road, with no other cars in sight. "I guess we aren't being followed," Pete said.

"I'm sure that we are on the right track now," Jupiter said. "With Hans and Konrad to back us up, I see no more obstacles."

They rattled onward, then turned onto the narrow road into Dial Canyon. Here the cliffs came close to the road, but presently it widened into the flat space where the house was built. Hans pulled to a stop. He called back to Jupiter.

"What we do now, Jupe? Somebody here ahead of us."

The boys stood up and stared ahead in dismay. The flat area held several large trucks, a bulldozer, and a giant diesel-operated shovel.

Just now the huge steel jaws of the shovel were chewing away at the house of Horatio August. Most of the roof and one side was gone already, for the shovel simply took large bites out of the structure and dropped the debris into a waiting truck. The bulldozer was smoothing the ground behind the house, ripping up trees and the remnants of a garden with the greatest of ease.

"The wreckers!" Pete exclaimed. "Mr. Dwiggins said the house would be torn down soon so that several new houses could be built here."

"And they're bulldozing the grounds to level them!" Bob groaned. "Maybe they've already dug up The Fiery Eye!"

"I think not," Gus said, frowning. "Look. The shadow of the mountain is over that way, on the lawn, and they're nowhere near there yet."

A truck full of debris from the house pulled up in front of them.

"Out of the way!" called the driver. "I've got to get by. We're on a time schedule on this job."

Hans pulled the salvage yard truck off the road and the other vehicle roared by. Already another truck was being filled with splintered rubbish from the fast-disappearing house.

"Drive on to that open spot," Jupiter called to Hans. "Then stop. If anybody asks us any questions, I'll do the talking."

"Okay, Jupe," Hans agreed. He drove the truck another two hundred yards and stopped where it would be out of the way. The boys piled out and stared at the remains of the house. A short stout man, dressed in a suit but wearing a metal safety helmet, came across the lawn toward them.

"What are you kids doing here?" he demanded, his tone unfriendly. "We don't want any spectators."

Bob and Pete had no idea what to say, but Jupiter had an answer ready.

"My uncle bought all the old furniture left in that house," he said. "He thought he might have left some so he sent us out to look."

"Nothing in that house!" the short man said emphatically. "Stripped bare. So turn around and get going."

"Can't we watch for a few minutes?" Jupiter asked. "Our friend—" he pointed to Gus—"is from England and he's never seen American demolition methods. He's very interested."

"I said get going," the man growled. "This is no circus. You kids might get hurt and our insurance doesn't cover that."

"Just for—" Jupiter took a quick look at his watch. It said two-fifteen. "For fifteen minutes?" he begged. "We'll stay way over here, out of the way."

But the man, who seemed to be the foreman, was not in an agreeable mood. "Now!" he said. "On your way!"

The boys all stared at the shadow of the peak that lay across the lawn. In fifteen minutes that point of the shadow would indicate the spot where The Fiery Eye was hidden.

"Yes, sir, we'll go," Jupiter said. "I'm sure you won't mind if I take one picture of the house, though. It won't take a minute."

Without waiting for an answer, he started for the point of the shadow on the lawn, adjusting his camera as he went. The foreman started to yell after him, then decided it was not worth the trouble. Jupiter stopped about a yard away from the end of the shadow, faced the house, and took a picture. Then he put down the camera and tied his shoelace. After that he came trotting back.

"Thank you, sir," he said. "We'll leave now."

"And don't come back!" the man said disagreeably. "Tomorrow we're bulldozing this whole place. In three months we'll have six new homes built around a central swimming pool. If you want to come back then, you can buy one of the houses!" And he gave a short laugh.

Jupiter climbed into the truck, and the others glumly followed him. Hans started the motor and drove slowly away. Pete sighed.

"That's rough," he said. "To be chased away just as we almost have our hands on Gus's inheritance. And tomorrow they'll bulldoze the lawn. We're licked."

"Not yet," Jupiter said, his lips set tightly. "We'll come back tonight when it's dark and try again."

"In the darkness?" Bob asked. "How can we find the right spot in the darkness? The peak won't be casting any shadow then."

"We'll ask the eagle to find it for us," Jupiter answered.

And with that mysterious remark, he refused to say anything more.

UNWELCOME INTRUDERS **16**

T I M E crawled past like a tired snail the rest of the afternoon. To make up for the time they had taken Hans and Konrad away from their jobs, Pete, Bob and Gus worked in the yard, painting a batch of metal lawn chairs so they looked almost new and ready for sale.

Jupiter spent the afternoon in the workshop section, fussing over some gadget he was devising. Just what it was he wouldn't say, but they guessed it had something to do with hunting for The Fiery Eye that night.

When the day's work ended, they all had dinner at Jupiter's house. After dinner Hans drove the smaller truck out of the yard. He parked it several blocks away in an inconspicuous spot, and settled himself to wait for them.

"Now," Jupiter said, "it is up to us to prepare a false trail in case anyone is watching us. I have phoned for the Rolls-Royce and Worthington to come as soon as it is dark. We must be ready for them."

"You're going to use up our last time to have the Rolls?" Pete asked. "Gosh, after this we'll be on foot!"

"We'll have our bikes and the use of the truck sometimes," Bob pointed out.

"That won't be enough," Pete grumbled. "Just when we need the truck for a case it won't be available. Mrs. Jones is getting pretty tired of us using it as it is. We're washed up as investigators."

"We'll have to do the best we can," Jupiter said. "It won't be easy, though."

Gus was interested in the Rolls-Royce and the manner in which Jupe had won the use of it.

"But now our time is up," Pete sighed, after giving Gus the details. "Jupe thought we had a lot more time coming, but Mr. Gelbert at the Rent-'n-Ride Auto Agency wouldn't listen to reason. So one more time and we're finished."

"That's too bad," Gus said. "Now that I see how vast this southern California region is, I realize how badly you need an automobile to get around."

"We'll try to think of something else," Jupiter said. "Now it's time to prepare our decoy. Everybody is to wear an extra jacket of mine out to the workshop. I have them here."

From the closet he got four jackets of different types and passed them around. The boys all struggled into them. They didn't fit too well, especially on Pete, but they managed.

"Lands and goodness, what game are you boys playing?" Mrs. Jones asked when she saw them. "I declare, I can't understand youth these days."

"We're going to play a trick on some, uh, friends, Aunt Mathilda," Jupiter said, and Mr. Jones chuckled.

"Just boyish pranks, Mathilda, dear," he said. "When I was a lad, I was full of such high spirits."

Jupiter led the way from the house back to the workshop section. The contraption Jupiter had been working on was lying on a table. It was a round metal object with a long handle, vaguely like a vacuum cleaner. A pair of headphones was connected by wire to the round metal section.

Also in the workshop were four of the dressmakers' dummies that Titus Jones had bought several days before. They stood in a row like headless soldiers standing at attention.

"Now we must dress these dummies," Jupe announced. "That's why I had you wear the extra jackets. If anyone is spying on us at this moment, I didn't want him to see us carrying spare clothing. Each of you put a jacket around one dummy and button it tight."

They did as instructed. When they had finished,

the dressmakers' dummies each wore a jacket with the sleeves hanging limply.

"They don't look very real to me," Pete observed. "That is, if you're going to try to fool anyone."

"They'll look better when they have heads," Jupe said. "Here are their heads."

He opened a paper bag and took out four large blue balloons.

"Each of you blow one up to the right size and tie it to a dummy's neck," Jupe said.

They followed his example. But even with balloons for heads, the dummies looked pretty sad.

"They'll look better as shadows in the darkness," Jupe said.

They waited. Slowly it got dark. The four dummies with balloon heads began to look strange and scary in the shadows.

A horn sounded in the salvage yard.

"That's Worthington," Jupiter said. "I told him to park as close as possible to this spot. Come on, each of us can carry a dummy."

Carrying the grotesque dummies, they filed through the piles of junk until the dark bulk of the Rolls-Royce blocked their way. Worthington had the door open, with the inside lights turned off.

"Here I am, Master Jupiter," he said. "Awaiting orders."

"These are your passengers, Worthington," Jupiter

said. "They are our stand-ins."

"Very good," the chauffeur answered. "Let me help them into the car."

Between them they got all four dummies into the car, leaning back against the seat. With the door shut and all lights off, all that could be seen were four shadows with bobbing heads. From a distance you could have imagined they were excited boys in the back seat.

"All right, Worthington," Jupiter said. "Now go up the coast road fairly rapidly, then turn into the hills and drive around for about two hours before you come back here and unload the dummies. Then I guess we won't be seeing you again. Our use of the car is up."

"So I understand," the tall English chauffeur said. "I'm sorry to hear it. I've enjoyed our association immensely. Very well, now I'm off."

"Drive out without your headlights. Don't put them on for a block," Jupiter instructed.

The boys watched him drive away, the car dark, just exactly as if trying to avoid attention.

"Well," Bob said, "if anyone's watching, I guess they'll think that's us. At first, anyway."

"I'm trusting any watchers will follow the car to see where we go," Jupiter replied. "Now it is our turn. We will all go out through Red Gate Rover and meet Hans and the truck. Pete, you carry my detector."

Pete picked up the long-handled object Jupiter had been fixing, and they all crept through the salvage yard to Red Gate Rover, some special swinging boards at the rear of the salvage yard. They slipped out into a dark alley-like street and trudged several blocks until they found Hans and the truck waiting for them in the deep shadows. They climbed in and started off. So far as they could see, no one followed them.

The trip to Dial Canyon was without incident. When they pulled up near the half-wrecked house of Gus's great-uncle, there wasn't a sound or a movement to be detected. Several big trucks were parked on the lawn and the bulldozer stood nearby, awaiting the next day's work. But fortunately there was no night watchman.

"After we get out, Hans," Jupiter told the driver, "turn the truck around and block the road. Keep watch. If you see anyone coming, honk the horn as a warning."

"Okay, Jupe," Hans agreed.

"So far, so good," Jupiter said, lowering his voice. "Now to see if my detector can ask the eagle for the right spot."

"I wish you'd explain what you're talking about," Pete said as they climbed out with the two spades and Jupiter's gadget.

"This is a metal detector," Jupiter said, taking the

instrument and leading the way across the lawn. "It will detect any buried metal several feet down."

"But The Fiery Eye isn't metal!" Bob objected.

"No, but when I stooped to tie my shoe this afternoon, after I took a picture of the house," Jupiter told him, "I shoved a silver half dollar into the ground to mark the spot. The half dollar has an eagle on the back. That's the eagle I'm going to ask."

"But it wasn't two-thirty yet, Jupiter," Gus put in as they walked over the lawn in the darkness. "Only two-fifteen."

"I made allowance for the probable movement of the shadow in the next fifteen minutes," Jupiter told him. "We shouldn't be too far off the right spot now."

He stopped and put the flat bottom of the instrument he carried on the ground. He put on the head phones, then snapped a switch and began to move the metal detector back and forth over the lawn.

"As soon as it finds any metal, it'll buzz," Jupiter said. "It's pretty dark but this seems about where I stood, judging by the house."

He moved the metal detector back and forth, over a wider and wider area. After he got tired Pete took over. Still it refused to buzz.

"We've lost the eagle," Pete said wearily. "This is just too big a lawn. We could spend all night looking."

"It has to be somewhere nearby," Jupe said. "I pushed it into the ground edgewise so it couldn't be spotted. Just give a swing over this way, Second."

Pete did as requested. Then he jumped. The machine had buzzed for a moment!

"Back! You passed over it," Jupe whispered.

Pete moved the instrument back an inch at a time. Presently it started to buzz loudly in his ears, and he let it rest on the grass.

"We've found it!" he cried.

Jupiter got down on his hands and knees and unclipped his flashlight from his belt. Holding the beam low to the ground, he poked around until he found his half dollar.

"Now," he said, "we have to dig. I might not be in exactly the right spot, so we'll make it a big hole."

Pete grabbed a shovel from Bob and started to dig. Slowly the hole grew deeper and larger. Except for the noise of the shovel, it was very silent in the canyon. Not even a cricket chirped.

They waited for the shovel to crunch on metal or wood—on a box of some kind—but it didn't. Presently Pete wiped his forehead with a dirty hand.

"I'm whipped," he said. "Jupe, I don't think this is the right spot."

Jupe said nothing. He was thinking intently. He looked at the dark shadow of the house, barely visible, then at the dark shadow of the peak, just visible against the starlit sky. Then he moved a foot toward the house.

"Try on this side of the hole," he said.

"Well, all right," Pete agreed. He jabbed the shovel in, and took out some dirt. Then some more. Then the shovel scraped on a stone. Or was it a stone?

"We've found something!" Pete whispered.

"Let me see," Jupe said tensely. He shone his flashlight on the spot. The corner of a small box, seemingly made out of stone, protruded from the ground. Jupiter knelt down and began digging around it with his fingers. Finally he got a grip on it. He wrenched and tugged, getting dirt all over himself. Slowly it came loose.

"We've got something," he whispered. "A box made of soapstone. Bob, shine my light on this while I see if it will open."

Jupiter began to fumble with the gold lock which closed the box. He shoved it first one way, then another. There was a little snap, and it flew open. Jupiter hesitated a moment, then slowly lifted the lid.

A blazing red stone shone like fire from its bed of cotton.

"We've found it!" Pete cried. "You did it, Jupe! You did it!"

"Well done, well done!" Gus exclaimed.

Jupiter started to answer. Then he stopped. All four of the boys stood as if turned to stone.

The night had seemingly exploded with brilliant light. The boys were in the center of four powerful flashlight beams. Almost blinded, they could barely see dark figures moving stealthily toward them from all sides.

"All right, kids!" growled a familiar voice. "Now you've finally got it, hand it over."

The boys blinked. Dimly behind the flashlights they could see four moustached figures closing in on them. One of them held a gun that looked large and menacing.

"The Black Moustache gang!" Bob managed to whisper. "They were here waiting for us! Hiding behind the trucks."

"We learned about your trip here this afternoon," the one named Joe said, "and how you got run off. We were pretty sure you'd be back."

"Never mind the talk. I want that stone, boy," the one called Hugo growled. "Hand it over now and no funny stuff."

Jupiter seemed more frightened than Bob had ever seen him before. His hand trembled. The stone box and the gem fell from his fingers into the hole.

"I—I'll pick it up," he said, his voice breaking.

He bent over, fumbled around in the dirt, and picked up the stone.

"Here it is," he said. "If you want it—take it!"

And he tossed the stone high over Hugo's head. It made a tiny crimson arc in the air and disappeared in the darkness beyond.

HUGO gave an ugly oath and spun around.

"Find it!" he shouted. "Turn your lights that way."

The lights all turned in the direction Jupiter had thrown the stone. Jupe gave orders of his own.

"Run for the truck!" he said. "Fast! They won't shoot."

He scrambled out of the hole. Like four rabbits, the boys bounded across the dark lawn to where Hans waited. Faithfully watching the road entering the canyon, Hans had not even seen the incident.

The Black Moustache gang was still busy looking for The Fiery Eye in the tall grass as the four boys reached the truck and scrambled into the back.

"Hans! Fast!" Jupiter shouted. "Get us out of here."

Hans asked no questions. The motor roared, the truck ground into gear, and a moment later they were thundering down the narrow road and away from Dial Canyon.

They didn't try to speak. They were busy holding on as the truck bounced and jounced around curves. Traffic was light and they made the trip back to The Jones Salvage Yard in record time. When Hans pulled through the open gate into the darkened yard, they climbed out glumly. They had left behind the shovels, the metal detector, and of course The Fiery Eye.

The boys clustered in a little group in front of the office.

"Well," Pete sighed, "that's that."

"They outsmarted us in the end," Bob said.

"Apparently so," Jupiter said.

"Apparently?" Gus's tone was questioning. "What do you mean, apparently, Jupiter?"

"I hoped they would be watching for the Rolls," Jupiter said. "They fooled us there. They were waiting at the house instead. Instinct told me to take added precautions. As a result—Bob, shine the flashlight this way."

Bob turned the flashlight beam on Jupiter. Jupe had his hand out, palm up, and in his palm glittered a brilliant red stone.

"Meet the real Fiery Eye," Jupiter said. "The one I threw away was the imitation stone Three-Dots left with us. I took it along, as I said, on a hunch. When I bent over to pick up the box and stone, I made a simple substitution."

"Jupe, you're a genius!" Bob said.

"I should say so!" Gus agreed. "You fooled them properly."

"I'll buy a double helping of that!" Pete exclaimed.

And then a voice, cold and quiet and deadly, spoke over their shoulders.

"And *I*—" it said—"will take The Fiery Eye now, young sir. Please hand it to me."

Before they could quite grasp what they had heard, the big yard light attached to the front of the office blazed on. The tall, thin man who had been standing unseen around the corner of the office stepped forward, holding out his hand.

It was Three-Dots. His sword cane swung in his other hand as if ready for use.

The boys stared at him, too surprised for speech.

"Don't try to run!" he said, raising the cane. He still held out his hand.

"Well," he said, "I am waiting. I have been waiting all evening. Your stratagem in sending away that highly visible Rolls-Royce with dummies inside was most amusing, but it did not work. I felt sure you would outwit those bunglers with their false moustaches and their babble about a bust of Augustus. I realized in time that the busts must be a false clue and I told them so. I deduced you were on the real trail. Now you have it. Give it to me."

Bob knew they were stuck now. Done for. The only

thing to do was give up The Fiery Eye.

But Jupiter still hesitated, the red stone balanced on his palm. He swallowed, then spoke.

"Mr. Rhandur," he said, "are you from the Temple of Justice in Pleshiwar?"

"I am, young man," Three-Dots said. "I am the contact with the world outside. For fifty years I and others before me have sought this stone so that our figure of Justice might once more judge good and evil. It was falsely sold by a renegade officer of the temple, who feared its power would reveal him. He suffered the consequences that befall all who steal the stone. Now give it to me before you, too, suffer the consequences."

He lifted the sword cane suggestively. Still Jupiter remained motionless.

"It has purified itself," he said. "It can be found, given, or bought, but it cannot be seized or stolen. That's what the legend says. I found it, so I'm safe. Now I'm giving it—to Gus.

"Here, Gus." He handed the ruby to the English boy, who took it, a little dumbfounded. "I've given it to you, so you're safe. But if you seize it from him, Mr. Rhandur, then it will be you who has to take the consequences."

For a long moment the tall man hesitated. His gaze was as piercing as an eagle's. Then slowly he withdrew his outstretched hand. He thrust it into the pocket of his coat.

"All along I felt sure I could frighten you into giving it to me," he said. "I was mistaken. You are right —I dare not seize it. However—"

He withdrew his hand, and in his fingers was a long green slip of paper. He extended it to Gus.

"I can buy it," he said. "You will notice that this check is certified. I was prepared to pay for The Eye if I could not gain it safely otherwise. You might sell it for more elsewhere, but again, you might never be able to sell it. Its history will haunt it and collectors will shy away from it. I advise you to take what I offer."

Slowly Gus took the check. He looked at it and his jaw dropped.

"Wow!" he said in good American fashion. "All right, sir, you can have it. It's a deal."

He held out the ruby. The tall man took it and it vanished into his pocket. He bowed.

"Fear nothing from those bunglers in the silly moustaches," he said. "They are mere opportunists who heard of Mr. August's hidden treasure and wished to find it to sell it to me. I regret my foolish efforts to frighten you into giving it up for nothing."

He paused for a moment.

"If you wonder what brought me here," he said, "it was the story in the newspaper about Mr. August's death. I have watched for years for some such item, and at last, belatedly, I found it. Now farewell."

He seemed to glide away like a huge cat. A car motor started up, then he was gone.

The four boys stared at each other.

"I feel like pinching myself to see if I'm real," Bob said at last.

"I'm too numb for pinching to do any good," Gus said. "This check—it's fabulous. What an inheritance Uncle Horatio left me! And you found it for me, Jupiter."

In a moment all three boys were laughing and shouting and pounding Jupiter on the back. But Jupiter just stood there, looking glum, not joining in the celebration.

"What is it, Jupe?" Bob asked at last. "You ought to feel like a million. What's wrong?"

"What's wrong?" Jupiter sighed. "Look at me. Dirt all over me. On my hands, my face, my clothes. And you know how Aunt Mathilda feels about dirt. The minute I go inside the house, she's going to make me take a bath."

Hector Sebastian Speaking

THERE'S not much more to tell about *The Mystery of the Fiery Eye*.

From the check that August August got for the ruby, he gave each of The Three Investigators a generous reward. The money went into their college funds. He also made a deal with Mr. Gelbert, manager of the Rent-'n-Ride Auto Agency, to guarantee The Three Investigators a car in the future. Worthington and the gold-plated Rolls-Royce will now be available to the firm whenever they're needed, and The Three Investigators can stay in business.

A few loose ends were tied up after the case was closed. Mr. Dwiggins wasn't a member of the Black Moustache gang, but he was responsible for the gang's getting a copy of Mr. August's mysterious message. Hugo, the leader, was Mr. Dwiggins' nephew. Hugo overheard Mr. Rhandur offering Mr. Dwiggins a lot of money if he could tell him where the Fiery Eye was.

Hugo forced his uncle to turn over Mr. August's

message to him. Mr. Dwiggins made up the story about being attacked because he was ashamed of having helped Hugo, even unintentionally. Hugo had been in the next room when the boys "rescued" Mr. Dwiggins, heard about the plaster busts, and guessed they were important.

Hugo then contacted Mr. Rhandur, who agreed to pay for the ruby if Hugo could deliver it to him. Hugo got together some disreputable friends, got Mr. Jackson's help, and began searching for the Fiery Eye.

This cleared up for Jupiter the puzzle of how Mr. Rhandur got the fake ruby so soon after Hugo found it in the broken bust of Augustus. Hugo had gone directly to Mr. Rhandur, who spotted it for a fake. Mr. Rhandur hinted that he had killed Hugo to get it just to scare the boys.

Gus has gone back to England with his inheritance. Hugo and his friends have made themselves scarce. As far as anyone knows, the Fiery Eye has been returned to its traditional resting place in the Temple of Justice in Pleshiwar, India, and all is quiet there.

As for The Three Investigators, they are again actively searching for a new mystery to solve. So, I wouldn't be surprised if they call me up any minute now. I'll be sure to tell you about their next adventure.

Have you read all of these exciting books in The Three Investigators mystery series?

The Secret of Terror Castle
The Mystery of the Stuttering Parrot
The Mystery of the Whispering Mummy
The Mystery of the Green Ghost
The Mystery of the Vanishing Treasure
The Secret of Skeleton Island
The Mystery of the Fiery Eye
The Mystery of the Silver Spider

And coming soon...
The Mystery of the Screaming Clock
The Mystery of the Moaning Cave

Available wherever books are sold!

• • •